For the cousins in Ireland –
Dylan, Harry and Shay

-JR

Published by Dragon Brothers Books Ltd
www.dragonbrothersbooks.com
© 2017 James Russell. Illustrations © 2017 Dragon Brothers Books.
A catalogue record for this book is available from the National Library of New Zealand. The moral rights of the author have been asserted. This book is copyright. Except for the purposes of fair reviewing no part of this publication may be reproduced or transmitted in any form or by any means, electronic or mechanical, including photocopying or recording, or stored in any information storage and retrieval system, without permission in writing from the publisher.
ISBN: 978-0-473-40633-2
Digital animations created by Courtney White
Cover illustration: Kerem Beyit
Internal vignettes: Suleyman Temiz
Chapter icon: istock
Editing: Rebecca Frazer

ARTS COUNCIL OF NEW ZEALAND TOI AOTEAROA

Produced with assistance from Creative New Zealand

THE DRAGON DEFENDERS

BOOK TWO

The Pitbull Returns

"Amazing! Once I started reading,
I couldn't stop!"
Jarvis Skilling, age 10

"So exciting!"
Liam Harvey, age 9

"Unputdownable! We can't wait for the next one!"
Dylan and Luie Townsend, age 8

"Can't wait 'til it's a movie!"
James Charlesworth, age 11

"A great book!"
Caleb Woodfield, age 9

A Dragon Brothers Book by

JAMES RUSSELL

www.dragonbrothersbooks.com

Sign up to find out when the next chapter book in the series comes out.

Simply visit **www.dragonbrothersbooks.com** and enter your email address. We'll keep you updated on new books, and we'll send you an email whenever anything cool happens!

Books in the series

Or, for younger readers

The Dragon Brothers Trilogy

The Dragon Defenders series grew out of The Dragon Brothers Trilogy – children's picture books for children aged 3-7.

How to use this book

This book is unlike any other you've seen. Of course, it works just like a normal book; you start reading at the start, and read right through to the end. That will work just fine.

But you can also enjoy it another way. You can download the free 'AR Reads' app onto a smartphone or tablet, point it at parts of the book and watch it become reality.

Your choice!

Here's how:

Step 1. Download the free 'AR Reads' app*.
You'll find this on the App Store, or on Google Play.

Step 2. Start up the app.

Step 3. Follow the set-up instructions.

Step 4. Point your device's camera at the pictures on the pages marked with a phone/tablet at the bottom.

*If you already have the AR Reads app downloaded onto your device, you'll need to check for updates in order for the app to work on The Dragon Defenders – Book Two. To use this app, your device will need to have an internet connection.

CHAPTER 1

The Pitbull's jaw muscles bunched and bulged as he chewed his breakfast.

"Delicious," he declared, taking up his napkin and carefully wiping the corners of his mouth. "I think I'll have them again tomorrow."

He had just finished eating a dozen tiny blue-green eggs, which had been stolen the day before from the nest of a very rare species of sea turtle in Guatemala. He'd instructed his chef to boil them for exactly two minutes. They were served with two slices of cold toast spread with French foie gras –

the mashed up liver of a goose. The meal cost an absolute fortune. Dining on the turtle's eggs brought that species one step closer to extinction, but it didn't

worry The Pitbull one bit – in fact, it made him feel important.

"Are you going to eat those?" said The Pitbull, looking up.

The Pitbull sat at one end of a long, black marble dining table. It was decorated in the centre with the head of a snarling dog, inlaid into the glossy surface in white stone. A shimmering array of fine silverware and Egyptian cotton napkins surrounded him. Fresh flowers bloomed from a vase and today's newspaper lay neatly folded to one side. Behind him, a floor-to-ceiling window gave an astonishing view of the city. The Pitbull's dining room and office were forty floors up.

The Pitbull's niece, Briar, sat at the far end of the table. She was staring down at her own plate of turtle's eggs, a look of disgust on her face.

"No," she replied, "I'd rather starve."

"They're very healthy – I think," he insisted.

Briar said nothing.

The Pitbull smiled. Sooner or later she would figure out what was good for her.

"How old are you?" he asked. "Nine? Ten?"

"Eleven," replied Briar.

"Whatever. In any case, it's time you grew up," said The Pitbull. "Your parents are dead. You're in my care. You'll do as I tell you. Now, eat up like a good little girl."

Briar looked at her uncle. Her long red hair – which shone like polished copper in the sun – fell like a curtain across her face, covering one eye. But it wasn't enough to hide the expression on her face – pure anger.

"No," she said.

The Pitbull rose from his seat. Slowly, he walked the length of the table. He stood directly behind his niece, towering over her.

He reached down, picked up her fork and held it out to her.

"Take this and eat your breakfast, you ungrateful little wretch," he hissed. "There will be nothing else."

Briar looked at the fork for a long time. Eventually, she reached out and took it. The Pitbull leaned over his niece, placing his hands on either side of her plate, palm-down on the table. She would learn some manners – by force if necessary.

Briar hovered the fork over one of the eggs. She looked straight ahead, and clenched her teeth.

"EAT! NOW!" he roared.

With the speed of a cat, Briar jabbed the fork into the back of his right hand.

"AAARGGH!" howled The Pitbull. "YOU SAVAGE LITTLE RAT!"

The Pitbull hissed at Briar like a viper.

"YOU WILL LEARN TO BEHAVE!" he roared. "YOU WILL DO WHAT I TELL YOU!"

The Pitbull's men came running at the sound of their master's voice. They had to restrain Briar, who flew at her uncle. The Pitbull hurriedly took a few steps backwards.

"Get her out of my sight!" he ordered. "Lock her in her room. Give her nothing for the rest of the day – no food, no water. Let's see how you like that, you animal!" Spittle flew from The Pitbull's mouth.

Briar kicked, bit and screamed at the men as she was dragged from the room.

When she was gone, and the sounds of her screams could no longer be heard, The Pitbull tried to sit still as one of his men bandaged his injured hand. But he was in too much of a foul mood. He pushed him away angrily.

"Leave me alone!" he commanded.

He grabbed the newspaper and scanned the pages, trying to take his mind off his troublesome neice. Eventually he calmed down. He began reading a story about a rare species of seabird that was returning from the brink of extinction. There was a picture of it – a plump black-feathered bird skimming above the waves. He wondered what it would taste like. The scientist interviewed for the story said it would be a long recovery process for the species.

'You can't hurry nature', he told the journalist.

But lately The Pitbull had been thinking exactly the opposite. His dragon's egg, which had been sitting in a specially constructed room in his private zoo for the past nine months, had shown no signs of hatching. He had spent a fortune on making sure the temperature of the room was just perfect. Another huge sum of money went towards making sure that the entire zoo was fire-proof, just in case the newly hatched dragon tried to burn its way out.

But the egg, which had been obtained at great expense, not to mention huge personal embarrassment, sat as still as a rock in his zoo. Day after day, he stared at it for over an hour, waiting for something to happen. But nothing did. Of course, he had no idea how long a dragon's egg normally takes to hatch. He also had no way of finding out – he certainly couldn't read it in a book.

What if, thought The Pitbull, he was to hit the egg with a hammer and chisel? To open up a small crack, just to help the baby dragon on its way?

The Pitbull rose from his seat. He was decided. He called loudly for his men.

"Get me a hammer and chisels and bring them to the egg room – now!" he barked. "Let's see if we can meet our little dragon – today!" He strode from the room, full of purpose. In the hallway, he pushed the button for the lift. It seemed to take forever, so he jabbed at it several more times. Finally it arrived, and The Pitbull stepped in. He told his men to wait for the next one, then descended the forty floors to ground level alone.

It was a long walk to the zoo through the endless rooms and corridors of The Pitbull's enormous home – giving him more than enough time to begin doubting his plan. What if putting a crack in the egg simply killed the baby dragon inside? Then it would never hatch and he would be back where he started almost a year ago.

The thought made him angry. He cast his mind back over the past year. He remembered when the pilot of his private jet first told him about the dragons. He'd seen some while flying over a remote island, five hundred miles out to sea. The Pitbull couldn't believe it. In fact, he'd refused to believe it. He thought the man had gone mad, and had him sent to the hospital so they could test his mind. But the man was released a week later, pronounced perfectly healthy, yet still telling the same story. The Pitbull sent another pilot and two photographers, in a smaller plane, to find out if it was actually true.

Within a month they had proof: dragons existed. Real, living, fire-breathing, roaring dragons. It was astonishing. Incredible. The stuff of dreams. The Pitbull suddenly saw his destiny – to be known forever as the man who discovered that dragons were real.

He'd thought it would be as easy as taking candy from a baby. The island was deserted apart from one family – a father and mother, with three young children – two boys and a girl. Nothing to worry about… or so he thought.

The Pitbull sent his three best men. He gave them orders to kill a dragon. He planned to stuff its body and display it in his hallway to impress his guests. He also ordered them to bring back a dragon's egg, so that he could hatch it in his private zoo.

Yet, when they arrived back three days later, they'd brought back only the egg. They had somehow been outsmarted by the two boys, who had stopped them from killing a dragon. He didn't bother listening to the men's excuses. In fact, it was only because they had successfully managed to find a dragon's egg that he didn't have them tied to a large concrete block and thrown into the deepest part of the ocean. He ordered the men to be held in his prison for three months as punishment.

The Pitbull's thoughts were interrupted by the ferocious roar of a huge male lion. The giant creature lunged against its cage as he entered the zoo. Row after row of cages lined the sides of the walkway, each occupied by one of the deadliest animals known to exist. A rare snow leopard was in the cage next to the lion, and then came a Bengal tiger. As he continued, he passed a cougar, a black panther, and a cheetah. Each threw itself against the iron bars as he walked by. The Pitbull smiled. His zookeepers were under orders not to feed the animals very much, so they were always angry.

Next came the large amphibians – a saltwater crocodile from Costa Rica, and a Nile crocodile from Egypt. Then came a huge alligator, and a gharial, which is from Nepal, and a black caiman from South America. Each and every one of them could bite off his leg and swallow it whole.

And so it went on – the twenty deadliest snakes in the world, and a section containing the fiercest of the small creatures – a wolverine, Tasmanian devil, and a honey badger. Further on was a large aquarium. Inside swam gigantic great white, tiger, and bull sharks. There was also a blue-ringed octopus, a box jellyfish, puffer and spine fish, and a host of other beautiful but incredibly deadly sea creatures. There wasn't a single animal in The Pitbull's zoo that could not inflict a nasty injury or bring about an early death.

The Pitbull felt right at home.

His men had caught up to him by the time he arrived at a room made completely from bullet-proof glass the colour of smoke. When The Pitbull

tapped a long code into a keypad outside the heavy door, the glass suddenly cleared, revealing what was inside.

As usual, there was no change in the egg. It sat on its stand in the centre of the room, oval and grey. Completely lifeless. It was as if it was a sculpture of an egg, carved from rock by an artist, rather than a real one.

The door slid silently open and The Pitbull walked in.

"Same as ever," he said. "Like a stone."

The Pitbull put one hand out to the side, palm upwards. He was expecting one of his men to rush forward and place the hammer and chisel into it, but instead they just stood watching him, wondering what on earth he was doing.

"You idiots!" he yelled. "The hammer! The chisel! BRING THEM TO ME!"

The man holding the tools rushed forward and gave them to The Pitbull.

"Get out!" he yelled. "Leave me!"

When The Pitbull was left alone, he began circling the egg. He looked carefully at its surface. From a few feet away, it appeared completely grey. On closer inspection, he saw little flecks of white, very like the tiny sparkles of quartz visible in river rocks.

"Where shall I crack it?" The Pitbull asked himself. "Let's start at the top."

Carefully placing the sharp blade of the chisel against the egg, The Pitbull tapped gently with the hammer.

"Easy does it," he said, concentrating fiercely on the task.

After five minutes of tapping, he moved in for a closer look.

"Not even scratched," he said with surprise.

The Pitbull raised the hammer a little higher and brought it down with a little more force.

Nothing.

"Harder," he said to himself.

He tried again, still harder.

Not even the smallest chip flew from the egg.

The Pitbull had run out of patience. Raising the hammer high above his head, he brought it down with all his might.

CLACK!

A violent vibration went through the chisel and up The Pitbull's arm, making his vision blur.

Again, he swung as hard as he could.

CLACK!

Again, the awful vibration. Pain ran up and down his arm. The fork injury on the back of his hand throbbed. Again, no visible damage to the egg.

"Damn you!" he yelled.

THUD!

"AAAAAARRRRRRRGGGGGHHHH!"

The Pitbull rolled on the floor, tears squeezing from his eyes. He clutched his finger. He had completely missed the chisel and hit the index finger on his left hand. His men burst in through the door, alarmed by his cries.

The Pitbull was furious. He yelled at his men to find a crowbar and a sledgehammer. He sent another man running for the first aid kit; his finger was bleeding badly.

While he was being bandaged, The Pitbull had another idea. He sent a third man to find a jackhammer – the kind road workers use for breaking through concrete.

When all was found and brought to the egg room, The Pitbull ordered his men to attack the egg.

First, they used the crowbar. It worked well, taking out small chips each time it struck the egg. But, by now, The Pitbull was tired of waiting.

"GET OUT OF MY WAY!" he yelled, taking up the jackhammer. With a vicious pull of the rip cord, the engine roared to life and the room filled with its smoky exhaust. The Pitbull ran at the egg with all the speed he could muster, holding the jackhammer up in front of him like a lance at a medieval jousting match.

The Pitbull's men leaped out of the way.

The jackhammer struck the egg right in the centre, its steel spike furiously battering at the surface.

There was an almighty crack.

The egg split right down the middle. The two halves fell away from each other, landing with a crash on the concrete floor.

Inside was nothing more than solid rock.

An inhuman scream of rage and frustration burst forth from The Pitbull, so piercing that his men scuttled away in fright.

CHAPTER 2

SPLAT!

Flynn hit the water flat on his belly.

Seconds later, he came up gasping for breath. He let out a long howl – his stomach was stinging like crazy.

From high above him, on the cliff, he heard a whistle.

"That must have hurt!" called Paddy. "But look on the bright side. You definitely broke the family record for the biggest splash!"

Flynn laughed, despite the pain. He swam to the base of the cliff and began climbing back up the sheer face. It was the third time he had attempted a double backward somersault, and the third time he had achieved only a sickening belly flop. He decided he'd practiced enough for one day.

"Wow. Look at that tummy," said Paddy, as Flynn hauled himself back onto the ledge. "I can see at least three different shades of pink, a little bit of purple and some red spots. It looks just like a beautiful sunset."

Flynn looked down at his aching stomach. The impact of his failed dives had indeed turned it a mottled pink.

"It must be your turn," he said to Paddy.

"No thanks," replied his brother, who lay back on the warm rock and closed his eyes. "I'm taking a nap."

It wasn't a bad idea. Flynn lay down beside Paddy. Just as he was settling, he heard a flutter and turned to see that Lightning, the boys' pet falcon, had landed on the ledge beside them.

"Squeee!"

"Hello to you, too," said Paddy, without opening his eyes.

The bird carefully folded his wings and looked at the boys.

"We've no food, I'm afraid," said Flynn. But he was pretty sure Lightning had just eaten, for the falcon seemed content to sit and rest with the boys.

Thankfully, the burning sensation on Flynn's stomach began to fade. It was a beautiful day. Below him, the water was so clear it was possible to see the reef fishes twenty feet under. A warm offshore breeze dried Flynn, leaving tiny white crystals of salt on his skin. He looked out to sea. Big rooster tails of foamy spray blew from the backs of the waves as they spun along the reef. Above him, the sky stretched clear and blue to the horizon. Just one cloud could be seen on this canvas of blue, directly above Mt Astonishing, the snow-capped volcano far to the east. Flynn looked along the coast to his right, towards the ever-growing heights of the Cliffs of Calamity.

It was as close to paradise as anywhere you'll find on earth.

He dropped his head back to the cool rock and closed his eyes. He let his thoughts drift, but as usual, they always returned to the same thing: The Pitbull. Flynn couldn't help but wonder if he had made a mistake by taking off the ties and straps that The Pitbull's men had attached to the dragon's egg and instead re-tying them to an egg-shaped rock. Then The Pitbull would have a real egg, and probably, by now, a real baby dragon. There would be no reason for him to return to The Island. On the other hand, Flynn couldn't bear the thought of a baby dragon held captive in a cage, deprived of its life here on The Island.

But it was too late for any of that. Flynn knew that now nine months had passed. The Pitbull would be growing impatient for his "egg" to hatch.

Although Flynn had never met him, he suspected he was the sort of man who would stop at nothing to get what he wanted.

He also knew that he would be embarrassed and angry at having being outsmarted by two young boys.

There was one thing Flynn was sure of: when The Pitbull finally discovered he had been carefully looking after a rock instead of a dragon's egg all this time, he would come back to The Island to seek revenge.

Flynn lay on the rock, worrying. But eventually the warm breeze and the soft sounds of surf on the reef and birds twittering in the forest worked their magic, and he drifted off to sleep.

The next thing he knew he was being roughly shaken by his brother, who was pointing out to sea.

"They're coming!" Paddy shouted, before launching himself off the cliff into the sea.

Flynn sat up in a panic, woozy with sleep. Instinctively, he reached for his slingshot.

He squinted in the bright sunlight. Finally, staggering to his feet, he searched the horizon, past the breaking waves. Then he saw it. A tiny white triangle on the vast blue of the sea. He breathed a sigh of relief. It was his grandparents in their little yacht, arriving for their monthly visit!

Flynn smiled. He stretched himself to his full height and tilted his head from side to side. His neck was stiff from the hard rock. He wriggled his fingers and toes, then stepped to the edge of the cliff. Taking a deep breath, he allowed himself to simply fall forward. His arms, at first outstretched, met over his head. This time he was in control and enjoyed the rush of speed as he plummeted downwards, diving deeply into the blue water.

"Yahoo!" he shouted as he broke the surface.

Up ahead, Flynn could see Paddy stroking back out to their canoe, which was anchored in the bay.

He was swimming fast with a freestyle stroke.

Then, Flynn saw him stop and tread water. He put his face under the surface. Paddy had seen something. As Flynn watched, his brother's legs went up in the air as he dived. Flynn took off, swimming as fast as he could. When he got to where he'd seen Paddy go under, he too dove and swam down. There was a thick forest of seaweed. Pulling himself through it, he searched for his brother. Finally, Flynn spotted Paddy's legs sticking out from underneath a large rock. He pulled hard through the weed, anxious to see what he had found.

Arriving beside his brother, he peered into the gloom under the rock. Without goggles it was a blur, but he could just make out two large orange-black blobs retreating into a crack in the rock – lobsters! Paddy must have seen them walking along the bottom. Now they were trying to escape.

Paddy shot out his arms. He managed to grab hold of both of them – one in each hand! He had cleverly protected himself from the lobsters' spikes with handfuls of seaweed. But now, with his hands full, Paddy couldn't push his way out. He kicked his legs furiously. Flynn could tell he was getting low on air.

Flynn backed out from under the ledge and caught hold of one of his brother's thrashing feet. Bracing himself against the rock, he pulled as hard as he could. Paddy came shooting out like a cork from a bottle and turned for the surface.

With a large lobster in each hand, both rapidly flapping their powerful tails, all Paddy had to do was point the creatures' behinds up towards the surface. The strength and speed of their flicking tails pulled him quicker than Flynn could swim!

The boys broke the surface and erupted with laughter.

"Lobster power," said Paddy.

"Nice catch!" said Flynn. "What were you going to do if I wasn't there to pull you out?"

"I had it all under control," said Paddy, smiling. "Lobster for dinner! Grandad's favourite!"

The boys threw the lobsters into the small canoe and killed them swiftly with their knives so they wouldn't suffer. Flynn threw a wet piece of sacking over them to keep them cool. Then, they took up their paddles and struck out for the reef. They could see their grandparents' yacht just entering Granny's Pass, the tight, twisting channel through the coral.

The boys' canoe could float in very shallow water and was able to pass right over the razor-sharp reef. But the keel of their grandparents' yacht hung down deeply into the water. They had to carefully steer through the channel to get to the calm cove inside the reef.

As usual, their grandfather had positioned himself at the bow. He was clearly in a panic. He peered over the side, pointing out rocks and coral to his wife, who ignored everything he said. The boys' grandmother could probably do it blindfolded if she had to. She winked and waved to the boys, and pointed at their grandfather with a mischievous grin.

The brothers couldn't help themselves; they cracked up laughing every time their grandfather yelled a warning about the next obstacle in the yacht's path.

"Hey Grandad!" yelled Paddy. "Look what's for dinner!" He held up the two lobsters.

"Marvellous!" said their grandfather. "That's super... watch out, love, for heaven's sake! You're going to hit that... oh, no you're not. Left a bit. Right a bit. Left... we brought some garlic, so we can make some... look out! Coral dead ahead!"

And so it went on. The boys were crying with laughter by the time the yacht slid into the cove. They paddled to the side of the yacht and jumped aboard, hugging their grandparents tightly.

Flynn dived over the side to check that the yacht's anchor was firmly buried in the sand, then they ferried their grandparents to shore in the little canoe.

Two exciting-looking wooden trunks came ashore with them. An emotional reunion took place on the beach, as the boys' mother and father and their almost four-year-old sister, Ada, came running out of the house to greet them. They all laughed when Clappers, the boys' horse, gave a loud whinny and came trotting down to the beach too.

CHAPTER 3

"What's this, Grandad?"

Paddy was rummaging in the bottom of one of his grandparents' wooden trunks. He held up a jumble of colourful wires and plugs, all connected to a book-sized, black glass plate. It was the strangest object he had ever seen. Coco, the boys' chocolate Labrador, sniffed it with interest.

Their grandfather glanced at his wife and a look of worry crossed their faces.

"Ah. Yes," he said. "We need to talk to you two about that. Do you have the phones you took from the men?"

Paddy nodded. His grandfather was talking about the smart phones the brothers had stolen from The Pitbull's men. Flynn had taken one from the mens' boat. The other they stole from Scorpion, the heavily muscled leader. While on the boat, Paddy had discovered how to use them. He tapped on one of the colourful squares on the screen of the phones, which activated its camera. Then, by chance, he held the phone over a page on which a coded message had been written. As if by magic, the phone decoded the message, revealing The Pitbull's orders to his men. It was how the boys discovered that the men were after a dragon's egg and were planning to kill a dragon. It also meant the brothers could stay one step ahead of them.

"They're here somewhere," said Paddy. He disappeared for a minute and returned holding a large wooden box.

"Just a moment," he said. He began to empty out the contents. His family laughed when they saw what he had collected: a full set of antlers, several prettily coloured stones, the skull of a bird, a collection of odd-shaped pieces of coral, and a number of half-carved pieces of wood and bone which Paddy had abandoned.

"I know they're here somewhere," he said, pulling out a leather satchel stuffed with feathers and a large conch shell, which he promptly put to his lips and blew. A low, droning sound came out, followed by a strangled squeak, which made them all laugh even more. He put it aside with a grin.

"I need a little more practice. Oh – here they are!" He held up the two identical phones. They were dusty from sitting at the bottom of the box and the screens were scratched. Both of the screens were black, and no amount of prodding at the buttons could light them up again.

"Why do you want them?" asked Flynn.

"Your grandfather and I have been thinking," replied their grandmother. "Sooner or later, I think we can expect another visit from The Pitbull or his men. Don't you?"

Flynn and Paddy looked at each other.

"They can try," said Paddy defiantly. "The same thing will happen to them."

"Perhaps," said their grandmother. "But we think you should be as prepared as possible. So, your grandfather built this." She pointed to the wire and glass contraption.

"The phones have batteries inside, which need to be charged before they'll work," explained their grandfather. "See this cord? Plug this end into those phones and leave the glass in the sunlight during the day. Point it directly towards the sun. The phones should charge – the glass is a solar panel and turns sunlight into electricity, which powers up the battery. It may be of no use, but perhaps it will help in case the men ever come back. Keep the phones charged at all times – you never know if, or when, The Pitbull's men will come."

Two days later, the boys and Ada lay curled in the hammock with their grandparents. They listened attentively as their grandmother read aloud from *Danny The Champion of the World* by Roald Dahl. They'd read it many times, and it was a favourite of both Paddy and Flynn's. They agreed that it might possibly be the world's most exciting book. Paddy often thought that the boy – Danny – was lucky to have a father like he did, because it would be terrible living without a brother or sister. He couldn't imagine it. But he loved the boldness of their plan to steal – or "poach" – all the pheasants from the estate of Mr Victor Hazell, their rich and horrible neighbour. It never failed to get his heart racing, even though he knew the ending to the book.

When their grandmother finished the book and closed the cover, there was a short silence.

"How come we don't live alone with our mother?" asked Paddy.

Flynn looked at his brother, a confused expression on his face. Ada sat up and looked at their grandmother, who smiled.

"Well, for a start, you need both a mummy and a daddy to make a boy such as yourself," she said.

"No," said Paddy. "I know that, of course. What I mean is, where did our father come from? Our mother is your daughter, but our father isn't your son. Where did he come from? Was he here on The Island already?"

Their grandmother chuckled.

"You mean to tell me you have never heard the story of how your mother and father met?"

The boys shook their heads. Ada looked from one to the other, then shook her head too. The boys giggled.

"I think perhaps the only person who has spent more time on this island than your grandfather and I is your mother," said their grandmother.

"She was born right here in the house. We wanted to go to the mainland so she could be born in the hospital, but there was a terrible storm and it was far too dangerous to sail. So we couldn't leave."

Their grandmother paused for a moment, deep in thought. "Do you know something? Since she was born, your mother has only ever left this island once, when she was about twenty years old. She had been begging us to take her to the city, to see what it was like. So, eventually, we took her.

"You should have seen her face – she was amazed, but also very frightened. She was shocked by the noise and speed of everything. She had no idea there were so many people in the world. She didn't like cars at all, and was nearly run over – twice! But, she was determined to walk around on her own, so we left her to explore."

Their grandmother told them that their mother felt overwhelmed, so she went inside a small café to escape the noise and bustle of the city. She ordered a cup of tea from the shy, sweet young man behind the counter. When he brought it over to her he spilled a little bit of it, but she didn't mind. They began to talk, and before long he put the 'closed' sign on the café door. The pair talked for hours, right through the night.

"We were worried when she didn't come back to the yacht," said their grandfather, "but, when she turned up the next morning, she brought that young man from the café with her."

While the children and their grandparents had been talking, the children's parents had come out of the house and were now standing beside the hammock, listening. Their father put his arm around their mother.

"Who was the young man?" asked Paddy.

"Blockhead!" said Flynn. "It was Dad!"

They all laughed.

"Your mother was like an angel when she came into my café that day," said their father. He gazed out to sea with a dreamy smile. "I was lonely in the city and looking for adventure. And, suddenly, there she was. Very beautiful, too, I might add," he said. He winked at his wife.

"I had saved for years to buy that little café, but when your mother asked me to come with her that morning I walked away from it without a second thought," he said.

Their grandmother smiled.

"Very romantic."

Paddy made a face.

"Then why did you and Grandad return to the mainland to live?" Flynn asked.

"I had responsibilities. I had to look after my own mother, your great-grandmother," she replied. "She was old and very ill. Also, our friends and families were there."

"Except for us," said Paddy.

"Except for you," replied his grandmother, and kissed him on the nose. "You're our reason

for coming back to The Island each month.
We wouldn't miss it for the world."

She stirred in the hammock.

"Come on, you," she said to her husband, nudging him with her toe. "It's time we were heading home."

Their grandfather pretended to be asleep, so the children leapt on him and tickled him until he cried out for them to stop.

An hour later, the little yacht was ready to go. The boys helped pack and stow everything away or lash it to the deck in preparation for their journey home, while their grandmother steered the boat though the pass. Once outside the reef, they helped pull up the sails and coil the ropes into neat piles. A stiff breeze blew, directly towards the mainland. To the west, the sun was beginning to set.

"You'll be home in no time with this wind," said Flynn. "By the time you wake up tomorrow you'll already be halfway."

Their grandparents hugged them tightly.

"See you in a month," said Paddy. "We love you."

"We love you, too," said their grandfather. "Now, do as I said – charge those phones and be alert. Keep safe."

"We will," said Flynn. "Come on, Paddy."

The two boys stood on the railing, blew a kiss to their grandparents, and dived off the side. They untied the rope tethered to their little canoe.

Their grandmother swung the tiller and hauled in the main sheet. The little yacht, catching the breeze, rapidly gathered pace.

"Goodbye boys," called their grandmother.

"Goodbye," they chorused.

As always, Paddy felt a tinge of sadness as he watched the yacht sail away.

Six hours later, the boys' grandfather stirred, woken by a low rumbling sound. He listened, and rose up on one elbow to peer out of the little porthole. In the distance he saw the dim lights of a passing ship. It passed by like a black ghost, he thought, and he shuddered involuntarily. It was heading in the opposite direction. Directly towards The Island. Rolling over, he went back to sleep.

CHAPTER 4

"What is our estimated arrival time?" The Pitbull watched the captain of the ship check his instruments, then double-check.

"We're on schedule, sir. We will be there exactly two hours before the sun rises."

"Make sure everything runs perfectly," snapped The Pitbull. "Update me every hour. If there are any mistakes I will hold you responsible. You'll be thrown overboard to the sharks."

"Yes sir. Very good, sir," the captain warbled. He was clearly terrified – just how The Pitbull liked it.

The Pitbull had not slept properly for three days. Whenever he lay down and closed his eyes, he was consumed by an incredible rage. He could think of nothing but the two boys who had made him look like such a fool. Nobody does that to The Pitbull! He would crush them. He would kill them. Or imprison them for the rest of their miserable lives. Nothing would get in his way. He had personally come on this mission so that nothing would be left to chance.

He went back to planning his mission and making encoded notes that would be read by his men using their phones.

The Pitbull had expanded his plans. For a start, he had purchased this ship – which he had named after himself. It was a beauty – as long as a football pitch is wide, and very fast for a ship of its size. Its deck rose forty feet above the ocean. The ship had belonged to the Navy, so when he got it, it was painted khaki green. He immediately had it painted black, with a white, snarling dog's head emblazoned on the side – The Pitbull's symbol. From the control room – the bridge – he could see everything.

This time, The Pitbull planned on catching four live dragons – he had run out of patience waiting for their eggs to hatch. Four large steel cages, designed especially to hold powerful, fire-breathing dragons, sat outside on the deck of the ship. He also had a crane constructed to move the cages around and on and off the ship, and had fire-proofed the entire deck. Down below, he had a huge cage full of live chickens and goats, which he intended to feed to the dragons on the voyage home.

Up near the front of the ship, on the deck, The Pitbull had instructed his men to remove the Navy guns to make room for two helicopters. It was a hard choice to make; he loved those guns, but knew he would need the helicopters. When The Pitbull looked through the window of the ship's bridge he could see them out there in the darkness, ready for action. These, too, he had painted black with the white dog. He had taken great pleasure in naming them after himself – Air Pitbull One, and Air Pitbull Two.

The Pitbull achieved all of this in just three days and at astronomical expense. When his panicking accountant told him that he had spent over eighteen million dollars, he threatened to feed him to the saltwater crocodile. His men, too, were exhausted. The Pitbull had forced them to work night and day to get the ship and helicopters ready. Apart from the captain and a couple of others, the rest of his men were now all fast asleep below deck in the ship's bedrooms.

The Pitbull heard a noise behind him. He turned. There was Briar, in her pajamas, her red hair tumbling across her face. She looked exhausted and it brought a smile to his face. It was 2.30am, and he had instructed one of his men to wake her. Since the fork incident, he had treated her extremely harshly. And now she had another lesson to learn.

"I'm going to run this entire operation from here," said The Pitbull. "I thought it might do you good to see what happens to children who disobey me."

CHAPTER 5

"*Squee!*"

Paddy ran towards the sound of Lightning's call as fast as he could, but he never seemed to get any closer to his pet falcon. He ducked under trees, crawled through thick bushes and waded through streams, but just couldn't seem to catch a glimpse of the bird.

"*Squee!*"

There it was again! Paddy changed direction and ran even faster. He struggled through a thick stand of trees. Thorns tore at his skin and pulled at his clothing.

Finally, bursting through the other side, Paddy staggered into a clearing in the forest. He stopped in his tracks. Lightning was being held in the tight grip of a muscular, tall man! An ugly scar ran down his cheek – The Pitbull!

"NO!" cried Paddy, and with the last of his strength, he threw himself at The Pitbull. As he did, he suddenly caught sight of a black object in The Pitbull's other hand – a gun! The Pitbull raised it, and aimed directly at Paddy. There was a flash of flame and a loud crack!

Paddy woke with a start. He almost yelled when he saw a face hovering right above his own! With relief he saw that it was Flynn, who was gently shaking him and whispering.

"Shhh," said Flynn. "You're just having a bad dream. It's OK. You're safe." Flynn smiled at his brother, then pointed. "Look – on the windowsill."

Paddy took some deep breaths to calm himself,

then he turned to see. Lightning was framed in the open window. His huge eyes stared intently at the boys.

"*Squee,*" the bird cried softly. "*Squee, squee, squee.*" Paddy realised he had heard the bird in his dream. He was glad Lightning was all right.

The boys were instantly alert – they knew Lightning must have seen something interesting close by. Three short cries was his hunting call. Without a sound, the bird flew away into the garden and returned a few seconds later.

"Squee, squee, squee."

The boys needed no further invitation. Careful not to wake their parents, they dressed and gathered their weapons. Paddy grabbed his bow and slung a quiver of arrows onto his back. Flynn took up his slingshot and a pouch full of smooth stones. They shouldered their backpacks and slipped out of the house into the cool of the early morning. Coco, who had been sleeping outside on the doormat, leapt about excitedly, licking the boys' hands.

"Wait a second," whispered Flynn. He ran back inside. When he reappeared, he had the two phones. Their grandfather's invention had worked perfectly – after only a day in the sun, they saw the little battery indicator on the screens go up to one hundred per cent.

"Good thinking," said Paddy. "Grandad said to keep them on us at all times." Flynn wrapped the phones in some waxed cloth and put them into his backpack.

Outside, it was almost pitch dark, windless, and silent. They would have to walk carefully – they didn't want to scare away whatever animal Lightning had seen.

A faint *"squee"* from above and to the east showed them the way, and without speaking the boys padded along, alert and ready for action. They worked their way into the foothills of the Mystic Mountains, following their falcon.

After an hour Paddy began to get grumpy.

"This better be a whole herd of deer. We've gone miles!" He was hungry for breakfast.

After another ten minutes of walking, the boys realised that they could no longer hear their falcon. His regular calls had simply stopped. Paddy searched the sky, but couldn't see him anywhere.

They climbed a tree and whistled, but the bird had vanished.

"This is ridiculous," said Paddy. "I'm going home."

Flynn agreed.

"He's never done that before," he said. The boys climbed down out of the tree and turned for home.

The sun was up by the time they reached the edge of the orchard. It had been planted many years before by their parents. No matter what time of year, there was always something to eat. Paddy couldn't wait; he pulled a nectarine off the tree and sank his teeth into it.

Flynn stopped too, and took a piece of fruit for himself. The two boys munched in silence, enjoying the sweet, juicy fruit.

Then, from somewhere in the distance beyond their home, came a faint, rapid, thudding sound. It grew louder and louder.

Suddenly, Lightning came racing through the orchard, twisting and turning between the branches like a feathered rocket.

"Squee!" cried the bird in a panic. In seconds he was gone again.

At the same time, from the direction of their house, clear as a bell, Paddy heard a man shouting an order.

With a deafening roar, two jet-black helicopters flew low over the orchard and away towards the centre of the island. Fear coursed through Paddy's body like an electric current. He fought the urge to run. Instinctively, he reached for his bow and lowered himself into the long grass. Flynn did the same. The boys had only ever seen helicopters in books; in real life they were far more frightening. Even worse, Paddy saw that painted onto their sides was the white snarling dog.

When the sound of the helicopters faded, Paddy listened carefully. There were more voices – all men. He could make out at least five different people. Then, above the sound of the men, he heard their mother shouting angrily: "Leave this house this instant! Go away!"

This was followed by the nasty sound of mocking laughter from the men.

It was all Paddy could do to control himself – every part of him wanted to burst from the orchard and attack the men in fury. Coco snarled. Paddy put his hand on her head to settle her.

Flynn wriggled over to Paddy on his elbows.

"We need to stay calm," he whispered. "We need to think."

"We need to fire some arrows into some butts," hissed Paddy.

"We can thank our lucky stars that we have such a clever falcon," said Flynn. "Lightning saved us by drawing us away. Come on – follow me."

Flynn commanded Coco to stay, then beckoning to Paddy, slowly got to his feet and began moving in a wide semi-circle. He travelled deeper into the forest, before doubling back towards the house. Paddy stayed right on his heels. At the rear of their home the forest grew almost up to the back door.

It was the best chance they had of getting close without being seen.

The boys moved as though they were stalking prey – one in front, one behind, not rushing, careful to step where there were no dry twigs or leaves to snap or rustle underfoot.

It seemed to take an age, but finally they had a good vantage point. Paddy could see five men surrounding the house, each holding a gun. They were guarding it, and he assumed that they were waiting for the brothers to return.

From this distance, Paddy couldn't tell if there were more men in the house. They must move closer.

Dropping to their bellies, the boys inched along the forest floor with great care. They reduced the distance to the house, but couldn't get any closer to hear what the men were saying. One of the guards stood at the back of the house, staring in their direction.

In desperation, Paddy looked around him.

Above the guard, high in the tree, sat Lightning.
He was as still as a statue. It gave Paddy an idea.

When Flynn wriggled up beside him, Paddy
whispered his plan to him. He saw Flynn's eyebrows
go up, but he nodded in agreement.

"Let's do it."

Moving slowly, Flynn reached for the leather pouch on his belt and slipped one of the stones out of it. Placing it in the pocket of his slingshot, he drew it back slowly and nodded to Paddy.

They would get just one chance.

Paddy nodded back, and Flynn let fly, away from the house and the men. The stone flew through the forest, thudding into a tree trunk and falling to the ground.

The men were quick and well trained. Hearing the noise, they raised their rifles and ran towards it at top speed.

The boys didn't hesitate. They sprinted the short distance to the base of the ancient tree at the back of their home and flew up its trunk. In seconds they were up in the branches, hidden by the thick canopy.

Paddy knew this tree well. They had played in it for many years, and could swing from branch to branch like spider monkeys. Hand over hand, he climbed the tall trunk, until they reached one of the largest of its branches. This particular branch, he knew, grew straight out from the trunk, before dipping down again towards the earth under its own terrific weight. It required the boys to walk along it, keeping their balance, for there were no smaller branches to grab hold of. As they moved along it, they drew level with the roof of the house. They hoped they'd be able to look in the windows.

Paddy, in front, felt a tap on his shoulder. He turned. Flynn had his index finger to his lips. Then he pointed directly down beneath them. Paddy looked. The guard had returned to his post, and was right below them! Paddy felt that at any moment he would hear them, look up and shoot them out of the tree like roosting pheasants in *Danny the Champion of the World*. Tiny shavings of bark from the tree, loosened by the boys' feet, drifted down on the man and settled on his cap and shoulders. But he didn't notice.

The brothers silently walked to the end of the branch until they reached the roof, gently climbing onto it. Then, as quietly as they could, they lay down so that just their heads peeped over the edge. The open window to the living room was directly below them. Through it Paddy immediately heard an angry voice that made his blood run cold. It was The Pitbull. No doubt about it.

CHAPTER 6

"**W**HY CAN'T YOU DO A SINGLE THING CORRECTLY!? WHAT IS WRONG WITH YOU IDIOTS?"

The furious voice of The Pitbull floated through the window and up to the brothers on the roof.

"Where are those brats!? Why aren't they tied up with the rest of their stupid family?" he demanded.

"I don't know, sir," stammered one of the men. "They weren't here. The rest of the family were asleep in their beds, but the boys' beds were empty."

His voice cracked and wavered as he explained himself to The Pitbull.

"You fools probably made so much noise you woke them up and scared them away. DAMN YOU!" he screamed.

"Sorry sir. We're so sorry," said the man.

"Where are you keeping the parents and sister?" asked The Pitbull.

"They're quite secure, sir. We have them locked in the bedroom."

"Keep them there, and remember this: if anything else goes wrong with this mission, I'll have you whipped!" yelled The Pitbull. "I'LL DO IT MYSELF!"

Flynn leaned over and whispered to Paddy: "I don't think The Pitbull is actually there in the room. Listen to his voice – it sounds like he's on the phone or something."

Paddy frowned.

"Then where is he? Back on the mainland?"

Flynn shrugged. He leaned forward and looked over the edge of the roof to check on the guard below. He was directly under the window, carefully scanning the trees.

"Hold my legs," Flynn whispered to Paddy.

Paddy sat on his brother's legs as Flynn wriggled far enough off the edge of the roof to get a look inside the room. There, on the dining table, sat a squat black box. A bunch of colourful wires and a handset were plugged into it.

The angry voice of The Pitbull came from the box. Two men sat in front of it. The man who had been speaking to The Pitbull leaned forward and listened carefully as his boss reeled off a long list of threats. Flynn could see that although he was a large, powerful man, he was shaking with fear.

"Nothing else will go wrong, sir. I have five men outside looking for the two boys right now. They won't be able to get within half a mile of the house without being spotted. The guards have instructions to shoot them with tranquilliser darts. Everything is under control, sir."

The Pitbull's voice came from the speakers in the black box.

"You'd better hope so. Now, connect me to the helicopters – I want to talk to my pilots."

Flynn signalled Paddy to pull him back onto the roof.

"The Pitbull is definitely not there. I think Mum, Dad, and Ada are safe – for now," he said. "But we need a plan… and quickly."

As Flynn spoke, the hopelessness of the situation dawned upon him. They were outnumbered, out-gunned and outsmarted. The guards had been told to shoot them. There was nothing they could do.

Once again, the boys heard the muffled thudding of a helicopter. In a panic, they prepared to leap back into the branches of the tree. But the sound had a strange quality to it, and Flynn realised that it, too, came from the black box on the table.

Here's your first opportunity to use the **AR Reads** app on your device (if you haven't downloaded it, you can find the instructions at the beginning of this book).

Simply start up the app, then point the device at this page and listen as The Pitbull is connected with his helicopter pilots. Make sure the volume is turned up. If you don't have a device – don't worry – just read on!

As the brothers listened, Flynn realised that The Pitbull had been connected over the radio with his helicopter pilots. They were on their way to Dragon's Crater!

Despite the danger of their situation, the boys couldn't help but giggle as The Pitbull became horribly confused talking to his two pilots. He was simply trying to get them to describe what they could see out of their windscreens, but when the pilot of Air Pitbull One replied "I can see the back of Air Pitbull Two" Flynn nearly laughed out loud. When the other pilot said he could see his own legs in front of him Paddy had to clamp a hand over his mouth and roll around on the roof.

But when the pilot of Air Pitbull Two instructed his gunner to get ready to shoot the boys fell silent. Flynn waited for the awful sound of a gun to come blasting through the radio. He dropped his head against his arm. Paddy sat in disbelief. They had failed all the dragons of The Island.

But that sound never came. Instead, Flynn heard the helicopter pilot say the most wonderful words he had ever heard: "There are no dragons, sir."

It took a moment for The Pitbull to understand what his pilots were telling him, but after a few minutes of listening, Flynn was sure: the dragons had left Dragon's Crater.

Flynn gave his brother a joyous, silent hug up on the roof of their house before quietly climbing back into the branches of the tree.

CHAPTER 7

"I don't get it. Where could they have gone?" asked Paddy.

It was only now that the boys had retreated to a safe place in the forest that he allowed himself to think about what had happened to all the dragons. The crater was their home, and there was normally hundreds of them, swooping and soaring and diving and breathing fire. Flynn told him it was a sight he would never forget, and he yearned to see it for himself. Among the dragons was the beautiful green male which Flynn had stopped

The Pitbull's men from shooting, by shoving stones down the barrel of their gun.

The dragon had then repaid the favour hours later, when Flynn and Paddy were facing certain death at the hands of Big Red – the giant dragon that lived in a cave on Mt Monstrous. He had swooped down on them at such speed that escape was impossible. Paddy and Flynn were in the centre of a clearing, and horribly exposed. Then, like a bolt from the blue, the green dragon had saved them, barrelling into Big Red's side with such force he had been sent tumbling to the far side of the clearing. It still thrilled Paddy to remember it.

Paddy and Flynn had spent the next few weeks afterwards talking of nothing else but the green dragon. They even gave him a name – Elton. Paddy had seen it on one of their parents' old records in the attic and they both liked the sound of it – Paddy thought it sounded like the note from a flute.

"Paddy, I think I know where the dragons are!" exclaimed Flynn, hopping from one foot to the other with excitement. He nodded to himself. "Yes, they must be. I'm right. I know I'm right!" He counted on his fingers.

"Flynn! Slow down! What are you talking about? Where?" said Paddy.

Flynn smiled at him and simply pointed to the east. Paddy turned. In the distance, the snow-capped peak of Mt Astonishing poked through the clouds.

"The dragon gathering! Remember? Grandad told us all about it. They're at Mt Astonishing! They must be!" yelled Flynn.

Paddy thought about this. It was a long time ago that their grandfather had told them the story of the time he decided to climb to the summit of Mt Astonishing. It had been a perfect, windless day, and he set off early in the morning. All had gone well, but as he progressed up the slopes of the mountain he noticed what he thought were birds flying around the mountaintop. He pressed on, and coming closer, saw that they weren't birds at all, but dragons, flying in a great cloud like swarming bees. He'd never seen them behave this way before. He watched them for an hour, mesmerised, before they all landed on the mountainside to rest. Paddy remembered his grandfather saying that it was the first time he'd ever seen them away from their home at Dragon's Crater.

But the following year, at the same time, he'd seen them again, this time rising up in a giant flock from Dragon's Crater, and heading for Mt Astonishing. They were like migrating birds, knowing exactly when to go, and where. It was then that their grandfather had realised that this was an annual event.

"It's too early in the year," said Paddy.

"Are you sure?" asked Flynn.

"Yes, I think so."

"Dragons don't have calendars," replied Flynn. "How do we know when, or how, they decide to hold the dragon gathering? It could be the moon, or the tides, or anything at all. Anyway, it's our only hope."

Flynn was right. Besides, they had no idea where else to look.

CHAPTER 8

The boys were interrupted by the roar of the helicopters' as they flew overhead and descended towards their home. The wind from their rotor blades made the branches of the trees sway violently as they landed. When the sound of their engines finally died away, Flynn realised there was another sound missing: birds. Usually the forest was alive with them, but they had been scared away by the men and the helicopters. It was deathly silent and it sent a shiver down his spine. With an effort, he forced himself into action.

"OK, there's one thing we need right away," he said.

"Breakfast," replied Paddy.

"What? No!" replied Flynn. "Well, OK, I guess we need to eat. So then we need two things right away. Breakfast – and Clappers. If we're going to Mt Astonishing, we need to move fast. We can make it there in under two hours if we ride Clappers."

"Good plan. You get Clappers, I'll get breakfast," said Paddy.

"What are you possibly going to get us for breakfast?"

"Leave that to me," said Paddy with a smile. "Don't get caught." He jogged away, keeping low behind a stand of shrubs.

Flynn went in the opposite direction, working his way slowly around to the far side of the house, where earlier they had seen Clappers. The men had tied her to a tree. Flynn moved closer, until he could see her, just beyond where the helicopters had landed. The poor thing was in a panic. Her island had been invaded by strange men and giant, noisy flying machines. Nervously, she pawed the ground.

Flynn moved from tree to tree, crawling and diving onto his stomach, creeping ever closer. He reached the woodshed, taking a moment to have a good look around. There were two guards, both facing in his direction. This was going to be tricky.

When one of the guards looked away, and the other reached down to slap at a mosquito on his ankle, Flynn ran hard for the helicopter and threw himself down beneath it. Clappers was now just thirty feet away, but right out in the open. Flynn had no idea how he was going to get to her. As he lay there thinking, he looked up at the helicopter above him. Flynn had read about them, but had never seen one. How were they ever going to fight against it?

The pilot had left the door ajar and Flynn noticed a flicker of white. It was a sheet of paper on the floor of the helicopter. A corner of it could be seen through the open door. It flapped in the breeze. With a quick glance to make sure the guard wasn't looking, Flynn reached up and snatched it. He smoothed it out on the grass. It was just a simple sheet of paper printed with a confusing jumble of letters and a single number. Flynn was sure it was a code of some kind. Quickly he folded it up and stuffed it in his pocket.

Suddenly, he heard the rustling of grass. He looked up to see one of the guards walking towards him! He must have heard something and was coming to investigate. Flynn froze. He wanted to run away, but found he couldn't move. Was he about to discover what it feels like to be shot?

Flynn could see the guard's feet moving slowly but purposefully through the grass, directly towards him. Clappers whinnied uneasily and shied away from the man as he passed.

Flynn suddenly found his courage. Carefully he took his slingshot from his belt and loaded a stone into it. Lying back, he pulled the stone to his cheek and took careful aim. He could see just the lower half of the man's body from under the helicopter, but if he could hit him squarely in the shin it might hurt him enough to give Flynn time to escape.

The man drew closer – he was just a few feet away from the helicopter. He stopped, and appeared to be listening carefully. Flynn's arm started to ache from holding back the slingshot for so long, but now he prepared to let fly.

"*Squawk! Bic-cawk! Bok bok bic-cawk!*" From the chicken coop, around the side of the house, came a terrible racket. Something had greatly upset the hens. Flynn saw the man's legs tense, turn, and break into a run towards the chicken coop. Now was his chance!

He didn't even look as he emerged from his hiding place. He simply rolled to his feet and sprinted towards Clappers. As he ran, he pulled his knife from its sheath on his belt. There was no time to untie the horse; he simply sliced through the rope, leapt upon the horse's back and clamped his knees into her sides.

Clappers needed no further encouragement. She sprang away like a greyhound and ran flat-out for the side of the house. As much as Flynn tried to turn her away, into the safety of the forest, she wouldn't be diverted from her course. As she rounded the corner of the house, Flynn immediately saw two guards, who turned in surprise at the sound of Clappers' flying hooves.

They had no time to react or raise their guns. Clappers hit them at full speed. The men bounced off her chest as though they were nine pins hit by a speeding bowling ball. It was all Flynn could do to stay on her back.

Clappers didn't slow down one bit. She rounded another corner of the house. The guard who had been standing beneath the tree was coming to investigate. He, too, went flying as Clappers struck him a glancing blow. There was a sickening crunch as he slammed into the house, knocking his head against the wall. He slumped in a heap.

At last Clappers turned for the forest. Flynn kept low, holding on around her neck, and urged her to even greater speed.

But they were not yet out of danger. One of the guards on the far side of the house had arrived in time to see his colleagues go flying. Flynn saw him calmly raise his rifle and train it on Clappers. He meant to shoot the horse!

At that precise moment, a miniature ball of feathered fury attacked him. Lightning dropped out of the sky like a brick, flew straight at the man's face, and wildly pecked and scratched with his powerful talons. At the same instant, Coco came barrelling out of the undergrowth and attacked the man's leg with a savage bite. The gun went off, but the bullet flew harmlessly into the ground. Just like that, before the man even knew what had hit him, Lightning and Coco were gone, racing after Clappers and Flynn into the forest.

Flynn let Clappers run for two minutes more – a mile or so – before he drew her up. She was breathing heavily from her exertions, so Flynn dismounted and walked a few feet away to better listen out for his brother. He began to worry. What would he do if Paddy had been captured? Coco soon appeared and happily lay down at Flynn's feet. Lightning fluttered down and settled on his shoulder. Flynn stroked the falcon's head in thanks.

He didn't have to wait long. A minute later Paddy emerged from the forest. He gave a toothy grin and patted their horse.

"Clappers! That was amazing! You skittled those guards! And Lightning! And Coco! You saved Clappers' life! What amazing animals!"

Clappers gave a soft whinny and pressed her warm nose into Paddy's hand. Coco woofed softly. Lightning simply looked from one boy to the other.

"Well? Did you get breakfast?" asked Flynn.

"Of course I did," said Paddy. "I got some fruit from the trees, tomatoes and beans from the garden, and some eggs."

Flynn laughed. "So, that was you – frightening all the hens in the chicken coop?"

Paddy smiled. "I wasn't sure how I was going to get away with that. But then Clappers came running around the corner."

Flynn shook his head. "Eggs?" he said in disbelief. "Raw eggs. How are we going to cook them?"

"Ah," replied Paddy. "You just leave that to me."

CHAPTER 9

An hour later, Flynn watched as his brother tried to keep half a dozen eggs safe while sliding down a steep, rocky bank. Somehow, he had managed to lose just a single egg on their entire journey so far. They had travelled through the Lunch Pass – a rough trail through the Mystic Mountains – and across the three rivers that fed into the Magic Terraces. The water reached as high as Clappers' chest in some places. They had been hurrying with great urgency, but hunger was biting at their stomachs.

"You're like a mother hen minding her eggs," Flynn said.

Paddy smiled.

"Breakfast time," he said, nodding towards a long, wispy line of white steam rising from a valley half a mile away. Flynn followed his gaze.

"The Boiling Stream!" exclaimed Flynn, suddenly realising what his brother had planned. "I can't believe I'm saying this, but you're a genius!"

"You're welcome," said Paddy.

The boys hurried to the Boiling Stream. It churned and tumbled, frothing over the rocks and then settling into deep, steaming pools. In the hottest parts of the stream the water was actually boiling; in others it was quite pleasant to swim in on a cold day. It was into one of the boiling pools that Paddy now lowered the eggs, contained in a little nest of flax.

As Paddy gently dropped them into the water, he began to count. "One, two, three…"

Flynn laughed.

"Why are you counting?"

"Don't interrupt," replied Paddy. "Eight, nine, ten…"

Flynn left his brother to the cooking. He sat down to rest. As he did so, he heard a crumpling sound from his pocket – the paper he had taken from the helicopter!

Carefully, he pulled it out and smoothed it flat on the ground. He concentrated hard on the code, but could make no sense of it. From his backpack he took out the two phones. He unwrapped them from the waxed cloth and pushed the buttons at the bottom. The battery levels had dipped a bit, but there was plenty of power left. He looked again at the coded message. It was unreadable – just random letters and the number four.

"Could it possibly still work?" he whispered to himself. He searched through the colourful squares on the phone until he found the red one with the letters 'AR' on it. He tapped it, and held it over the paper.

QBYEXN MBOG WSCCSYX:

4 NBKQYXC KBO DY LO
DKUOX KVSFO

CRYYD DROW GSDR
DBKXA ESVVSCOB NKBDC.
DRO OPPOMDC GSVV VKCD
PYB DGY RYEBC.

DBKXCZYBD DROW DY DRO
MKQOC YX DRO CRSZ.

NY XYD PKSV.

Dro Zsdlew

Here's your second opportunity to use
the **AR Reads** app on your device (if you
haven't downloaded it, you can find the
instructions at the beginning of this book).
Simply start up the app, then point the
device at this page and watch as the code
reveals itself! If you don't have a device –
don't worry – just read on!

Flynn's eyes widened as he read The Pitbull's message.

"Paddy!" he yelled. "Come and see this! Quick!"

"Don't interrupt me! I'll lose count... one hundred and twenty three, one hundred and twenty four..."

"Never mind the eggs!" shouted Flynn. "You have to see this."

Grumbling, Paddy walked over to take a look.

"Hey, it's a code!" he exclaimed. "Where did you get that?"

"I took it from one of the helicopters," replied Flynn. "Look what it says."

Flynn held the phone over the page and Paddy read out loud as the random letters rearranged themselves into a message.

"Four dragons are to be taken alive. Shoot them with tranquilliser darts. What's a tranquilliser dart?"

"I've read about them," said Flynn. "They don't kill the animal. They just put them to sleep for a while. They're used on dangerous animals – like lions or tigers."

Paddy continued. "The effects will last for two hours. Transport them to the cages on the ship. Do not fail. The Pitbull."

Paddy punched the ground in rage and frustration.

"How are we supposed to stop this?" he cried. "We don't have a chance. What are we even doing here? Are we planning on telling the dragons to fly away? We should be at home, trying to rescue our parents and sister!" He stood up and angrily kicked at the old, rotten trunk of a tree. Chunks of brittle wood flew everywhere.

Flynn walked over to his brother and put his hand on his shoulder.

"I know," he said. "I've been thinking the same thing. You're right. Perhaps we're better off letting The Pitbull win and catch his four dragons. Then he might leave us alone."

"So, we go home, turn ourselves in to the guards, and wait until they've completed their mission?" said Paddy.

"I guess so," replied Flynn. "But let's eat first."

Miserably, Paddy walked over to the boiling stream and pulled his eggs from the water. The boys sat in silence, eating the over-cooked eggs and munching on tomatoes and raw beans. The realisation that The Pitbull was going to succeed, and the thought of four dragons living the rest of their lives in a zoo made Flynn's lunch taste very sour indeed. Even Coco seemed disinterested in her egg.

When they were finished, the boys re-packed their rucksacks and prepared to go. As they mounted Clappers, they heard a distant roar from the direction of Mt Astonishing. Flynn turned to see the tiny dark forms of dragons swooping around the craggy peaks of the mountain.

"You were right," said Paddy. "The dragons are at Mt Astonishing. It's only a matter of time until The Pitbull's men find them."

Sadly, the boys turned away. Paddy gave Clappers' belly a gentle nudge with his heels.

She seemed reluctant to move, but eventually set off in the direction of home.

CHAPTER 10

"YOU DID WHAT? YOU LET THEM ESCAPE? AGAIN? WHEN THIS IS ALL OVER YOU'RE GOING FOR A SWIM IN THE PIRANHA TANK!"

The Pitbull was furious. He could feel his face heating up and the veins throbbing in his neck. His right eye twitched uncontrollably. Grabbing the handpiece of the radio, he ripped it out of the machine and smashed it on the edge of the desk until it broke into pieces. A sharp shard of plastic dug into the palm of his hand.

"ARRGGHH!" he yelled. In a fury, he pushed the whole radio onto the ground. He then jumped up and down on it until it lay in a hundred pieces.

He heard a noise behind him and spun around. Briar was watching him, trying to hide a smile.

"You seem tense," she said.

"Tense? TENSE?" he replied. "Are you trying to be funny? I'll have you thrown into the engine room for the rest of the mission!"

Briar shook her head.

"Not at all. All I'm saying is that perhaps it's just not meant to be."

The Pitbull couldn't believe what he was hearing.

"Not meant to be? What does that mean?"

Briar looked thoughtful.

"I mean that maybe people aren't supposed to keep dragons in captivity. Perhaps the world is trying to tell you, but you refuse to listen."

The Pitbull gritted his teeth and bent down so that his face almost touched Briar's. He spoke very quietly.

"The world does whatever I want it to. The world is here for people like me to control. I bend it to my will. If I want a dragon – if I want four dragons – in my zoo, then I will have them. Nothing – or nobody – will stand in my way."

Briar shrugged. "OK, whatever. But you've got a problem… there are no dragons."

The Pitbull stood and turned away from her. She was right, but he didn't want to admit it. He stared out of the bridge window, looking across the sparkling blue sea, thinking. Then, it came to him. He nodded slowly and a smile crossed his lips. He knew what to do.

The Pitbull turned back to the radio, ready to give an order. He'd forgotten it was no longer on the desk, but on the floor in tiny bits and pieces.

"GET ME A NEW RADIO!" he roared, and his men scattered in all directions. "Send the order to the helicopters to fly a grid pattern over the whole island until they spot them. A hundred dragons can't have disappeared into thin air!"

CHAPTER 11

Paddy felt worse with every step they took towards their home. He was at a complete loss. In order to keep their family safe, there was simply nothing else he could think of to do. Their mum, dad and sister were more important than four dragons. He realised their only hope was to give up and let The Pitbull win.

Paddy felt better talking about it, but Flynn didn't speak, seemingly lost in his thoughts.

"What if one of the dragons they catch is Elton?" said Paddy. "What if they take him away?"

He couldn't bear to think of the beautiful green dragon, lost forever, imprisoned in a cage. "Please don't let them catch Elton," he said aloud, over and over.

Paddy felt Flynn lean back slightly, which was the signal for Clappers to stop. The horse pulled up and stood quietly, waiting.

"What's up?" said Paddy. "Why are we stopping?"

Flynn stared straight ahead, without speaking. Suddenly he turned, and looked back towards Mt Astonishing.

"What is it?" asked Paddy.

Flynn said nothing for a moment, but Paddy saw a defiant flash in his brother's eyes. Then, a slow smile spread across his face.

"I have an idea," said Flynn. "It's crazy, but it just might work. Come on, I'll tell you on the way."

"Yes!" Paddy cried excitedly, as Flynn turned Clappers back towards Mt Astonishing and urged her to a thunderous gallop.

CHAPTER 12

Great torrents of water crashed down on Flynn's head. He held his breath and climbed, struggling to hold onto the slippery rocks. Slowly, and with great care, he moved upward, hand over hand, through the freezing, foaming water. Sometimes, it was impossible to see where he was going – he had to climb by touch alone.

He and Paddy were halfway up the Fairy Falls, a series of waterfalls which tumble down the side of Mt Astonishing for over five hundred vertical feet. Flynn had often marvelled at their beauty, but never believed he'd attempt to climb them.

Paddy yelled out in alarm, almost losing his grip on the slippery rock.

"Did we really have to go this way?"

Flynn said nothing. They both knew that there were easier routes up Mt Astonishing, but they couldn't risk being seen by the dragons. By climbing up Fairy Falls, they could stay out of sight.

At the base of the falls, they had sent Clappers and Coco home, and Flynn was now feeling quite alone.

When they finally reached the top, he collapsed beside Paddy on a sunny rock, totally exhausted. His fingers were numb and he had a terrible case of brain freeze.

Eventually, the sun began to warm his body. He and Paddy climbed the low rocky bank just above them to take a look around. As they pulled themselves up, they were met with the most incredible sight. The Island's entire population of dragons wheeled and soared around the mountaintop and dived through the valleys at speed. It was a beautiful spectacle against the dazzling white snow. The dragons' colourful skin sparkled in the sunlight. Occasionally, a dragon would send a super-heated fireball into the deep snow, where it instantly vaporised the frozen water into a tremendous column of rising steam. Immediately, all the other dragons raced to fly through the cloud. It appeared to be some sort of game and the dragons' joyful roars echoed around the mountain slopes. The boys simply watched in wonder without saying a word to each other.

Flynn heard a *"squee"* and turned to see that Lightning had arrived. He landed gracefully on a rock, then immediately launched himself off again. He flew a short distance to the northwest, turned, and came back to the rock. He repeated this three more times. Flynn gazed past the falcon to the horizon. It was then that he saw them in the distance; two tiny black shapes, flying north. The helicopters! They flew almost out of sight, then turned and came south again, though this time a little more to the east, closer to Mt Astonishing. They were searching The Island!

"We have to move," said Paddy. "Quickly!"

Flynn gulped. They had a daunting task before them. They now had to scale a narrow ridge, while staying out of sight of the scores of dragons above them and across the valley.

They set off, keeping low and scrambling behind rocks. It was a frightening experience. The dragons' screeches hurt Flynn's ears and he could feel the heat from their fire as they passed overhead.

Half an hour later, they had reached their goal – an overhanging rock from where they could watch the dragons, while staying out of sight. Together, the boys lay down and scanned the mountainside.

Suddenly, Paddy gave a joyous shout.

"There!" he yelled, pointing to a rock platform, half way up a huge cliff, on the far side of the valley.

Flynn's heart beat wildly. They had found him. They had found Elton!

CHAPTER 13

The boys climbed for more than an hour to reach the other side of the valley. They scrambled across frozen waterfalls and fought their way through deep snow, all the time trying to stay out of sight of the dragons wheeling in the sky above them. Paddy saw that they had reached the monstrous cliff where they had spotted Elton.

He saw that the next part would be tricky, and very dangerous. With great care, they inched their way along a thin ledge that cut across the face of the cliff. Frozen and exhausted, Paddy's legs and arms shook with the effort.

Their trail ran right up against the cliff, and he could no longer see Elton. For all he knew, he may have already taken to the sky and be miles away by now.

He could see the helicopters, no more than four or five miles distant. They flew backwards and forwards across The Island, coming closer and closer.

Paddy led, Flynn followed. They clung to any handhold they could find on the cliff face. Most of them weren't handholds at all – more like tiny lumps or cracks in the smooth rock. It was incredibly dangerous. One slip, and the brothers would fall a thousand feet to their deaths.

Finally, as they neared the end of the ledge, the rock platform where they had seen Elton was slowly revealed. As he shuffled the last few feet, Paddy saw the tip of a long, graceful tail. It was the colour of a polished emerald. Elton's tail! He was still there! Paddy hurried, anxious to see the incredible green dragon again. Fear pricked at the back of his skull. What if the dragon didn't recognise them? What if he did, and attacked anyway? There were so many what-ifs, but they were committed now. Come what may, Paddy was determined to see this through.

Glad to be off the tiny ledge, Paddy walked onto the rock platform to finally stand in front of the dragon. The sight of him took his breath away.

Now that he was up close, Paddy could see what a truly enormous animal Elton was. His bright green scales seemed to glow against the vivid orange of his colossal wings, which were gracefully folded to the sides of his body. His legs were long and muscular, boasting talons that looked like they could crush rocks. His noble head was long and streamlined, with clusters of spines raked backwards over his powerful neck. Puffs of white smoke billowed from his nostrils. Paddy heard a deep, low rumble; the dragon was sound asleep and snoring heavily.

This, of course, made the boys giggle.

As the brothers stood in wonder, mesmerised by this beautiful dragon, Paddy became aware of another presence. Something was moving behind Elton. He heard the sound of rocks clunking together and the unmistakable throaty snort of a large animal.

Alarmed, he looked at Flynn.

"What is it?" Paddy hissed.

Flynn shrugged his shoulders and put his finger to his lips. He motioned for Paddy to get down. But there was nowhere to hide.

As they stood, transfixed, another dragon slowly appeared from behind Elton. It was obviously a female, with a finer, more slender head. She was huge. She had cobalt blue skin and luminous yellow wings. She rose up and craned her neck to the sky, turning her head away from the boys, towards the sun. Her eyes were closed against the glare. She looked to be enjoying a good stretch after waking from a deep sleep. Then, she spread her wings out as wide as they could go. They were so large that Paddy suddenly felt as though he was inside a cavernous tent. The sun lit up the thin, translucent skin covering her wings and bathed the rock platform in a butter-coloured, glowing light.

Paddy was stuck to the ground with fear. He did the only thing he could think of – reach for his weapon.

Paddy notched an arrow to the string of his bow and saw Flynn reaching for a stone for his slingshot. But his brother fumbled, and the stone fell from the pouch, landing with a soft "clunk" on the ground.

The relaxed, cat-like movements of the female dragon changed in an instant. She tensed and her muscles bulged. The spines on her neck sprung out like the hackles rising on a dog. Her huge head swivelled. Her deep green eyes flicked open and fixed upon the boys. In one swift and powerful movement, she stepped across Elton and let forth a screaming roar so powerful that the boys staggered backwards in horror, towards the edge of the cliff.

CHAPTER 14

"**M**y mother would never have let you do this."

Briar stood in the bridge of The Pitbull's ship, her feet apart, staring hard at him. She had a defiant look on her face, which both amused and irritated The Pitbull.

"Your mother is dead," replied The Pitbull.

He was waiting to hear an update on the search for the dragons. But the new radio lay silent. His helicopter pilots had been searching The Island for almost two hours, with nothing to show for it.

"You don't have to do this," said Briar. "You could just turn around and go home right now and leave the dragons on The Island. They're wild animals. They probably won't survive if you lock them up."

He'd heard enough.

"You don't know what you're talking about. Why don't you shut up and stop bothering the adults?"

He saw the girl's eyes flash with anger.

"Don't talk to me like that!" she yelled. "I know more about nature and animals than you do!"

The Pitbull glared at her.

"You're a kid. In fact, you're a brat who knows nothing of the world. And I'm the fool who gets to raise you because your stupid parents went and got themselves killed. Lucky me."

Briar screamed at him.

"Don't you dare call them stupid!"

He laughed, enjoying the look on her face.

"I will call them whatever I want. And you will do what I tell you. Take her away."

This last order was given to one of his men, standing at the doorway. He came forward and grabbed Briar roughly. Seconds later, he was lying on the ground with a stream of blood trickling out of his nose and a wobbly front tooth. Briar marched from the room.

"You're an embarrassment," The Pitbull said to the man. "Tripped up by a little girl. Get out of my sight."

As the man left the room, the radio suddenly crackled into life.

"Pitbull Command, come in, over."

The Pitbull ran to the radio and snatched up the receiver.

"This is Pitbull Command. Who's this?"

There was a long silence. The Pitbull erupted.

"I said WHO IS THIS?"

More silence.

Finally the radio came alive again.

"Sir, are you talking to me, sir? Over."

"Of course I'm talking to you."

"You have to say 'over', then I know you've finished speaking, sir. Over."

"What?"

The radio was once again silent.

The Pitbull sighed.

"OK, I get it. Give me a progress report. Over. OVER!"

"Sir, you only have to say it once, over."

"I'LL SAY IT AS MANY TIMES AS I LIKE! NOW GIVE ME A PROGRESS REPORT, OVER!"

"Sir, are you asking Air Pitbull One, or Air Pitbull Two, sir? Over."

"EITHER OF YOU! WHOEVER CAN SEE WHAT'S GOING ON! OVER!"

The Pitbull listened with a growing sense of disappointment as his pilots told him that once again they had found nothing. Suddenly he felt like a fool. A fool for spending millions on this mission, when it looked likely that he was going home empty handed

– again! It made him very angry indeed. He blamed the brothers – they must have lured the dragons away somehow. He put his head in his hands.

"Sir? Do you copy? Over. Sir, are you still there?"

The Pitbull snapped out of his thoughts. He'd been thinking about what he would do to the boys if he ever caught them.

"Sir, I think I can see… is it? Yes… I think it is… no, perhaps not… no, wait, yes it is. It is, sir!" stammered the Air Pitbull One pilot.

"What on earth are you saying, you idiot?" asked The Pitbull. He leaned closer to the speaker, excited about what his pilots may have seen.

"Sir, I do believe we've found… yes, we have definitely found…"

"What? WHAT?" yelled The Pitbull.

"We have found the dragons, sir! Over!"

"YEESSS!" The Pitbull punched the air.

His pilot continued in an excited voice.

"There must be fifty of them, or a hundred – it's

impossible to tell. They're flying in all directions, sir. Near the top of the mountain. Over."

After the ridiculous experience of trying to communicate with his pilots that morning, The Pitbull had ordered his engineers to fit cameras both inside and outside of the helicopters. He also had them install a screen in the cockpit so that his pilots could see him too.

"Turn on your cameras! I want to see!" he yelled.

"Stand by for visual, sir. Over," said the pilot.

The Pitbull raced to the screen. He stabbed at some buttons, but had no idea how to use it. He called for Briar, but then remembered she had stormed out. He roared at the captain, who hurriedly set to work. Before long, a clear picture appeared.

The view was of the craggy peak of Mt Astonishing. At first, The Pitbull could see only the mountaintop. Then, he spotted them – at this distance they were just tiny specks flying around the peaks and valleys. But as the helicopter drew closer, he could make them out more clearly, and he caught his breath. There were scores of dragons, swooping and climbing, banking and gliding. Some were high in the sky, others almost skimmed the ground. They were magnificent flyers. They had an incredible elegance, like an albatross gliding across ocean swells.

Suddenly, The Pitbull could see his future very clearly. He would capture many of these magnificent creatures and house them in a giant, purpose-built enclosure. He would be the most famous man in history! In time, he would come to be known as 'The Dragon Keeper', or perhaps 'The Dragon Master'.

The Pitbull was trying to decide which sounded better when he saw something strange on the screen. On a rock platform, halfway up a cliff overhanging a vast valley, he saw the distant forms of two people. Yes, it definitely was! He could just make them out. As the helicopter came closer, he realised they were children – two boys! He could see them cowering and stumbling backwards,

obviously afraid of something. Whatever it was,
The Pitbull couldn't see it; it was hidden by an
outcrop of rock.

As he watched, the two boys retreated backwards,
right to the edge of the cliff. The Pitbull saw the
smaller boy lift his bow and draw an arrow back
to his cheek. The older boy aimed his slingshot.
They must have heard the sound of the helicopters
because they both turned and looked towards

the camera for an instant, before turning back to whatever was coming at them. The Pitbull recognised them immediately – it was the brothers!

Then, The Pitbull saw what they were so afraid of. A smile spread across his face. Slowly, from behind the rock, advancing across the platform, came a gigantic and ferocious-looking dragon. Its body was the bright blue of a sapphire, its wings the colour of the noonday sun. The creature's mouth was wide open, revealing rows of razor-sharp teeth.

Plumes of smoke from its nose made the frosty air shimmer in the intense heat. Now, even through the lens of the camera, The Pitbull could see the white-hot glare of a fireball forming at the back of the creature's throat.

"Get closer," he instructed the pilot. "I'm going to enjoy this."

The Pitbull pulled up a chair and sat to watch the show.

CHAPTER 15

The heat from the dragon's mouth was incredible, and she had yet to launch her fireball.

Paddy fired an arrow. It harmlessly glanced off the dragon's bony head. The stone from Flynn's slingshot may as well have been a pea for all the harm it caused. The shots only made her angrier.

The boys had retreated as far as they could go and were now teetering on the edge of the cliff. Behind them, over the edge, was a thousand feet of dizzying free-fall, then instant death on the rocks below.

That fate was just seconds away.

The fireball grew and grew. The dragon must surely send it blazing towards them at any moment. Paddy cried out in terror, but Flynn remained silent and simply bowed his head. He couldn't believe that it had come to this – death on Mt Astonishing. Death by a creature they were trying to protect. The entire dragon population of The Island was now in danger. Now, no one would save them.

At the very moment he expected to be blown clean off the cliff in a firestorm of flame and scorching wind, Flynn heard an almighty crack and felt a fierce heat off to one side. The dragon's fireball had missed! Then came a series of roars so loud they threatened to burst his eardrums.

Flynn spun around. It was an astonishing sight! A thrashing tangle of teeth, talons, beating wings and whipping tails. Elton had awoken, and he was furiously fighting the female dragon, trying to drag her away from the brothers. She roared in anger and sent fireball after fireball shooting up into the sky.

The brothers watched in fearful awe. The two dragons rolled over and over, clasped in a deadly embrace. Eventually, Flynn could see that Elton was the stronger of the two and slowly gaining the upper hand, but not without a fierce and tiring fight.

Finally, Elton pinned down the female. She was unable to move under his huge weight and strength. He roared into her face until she laid back her head, conceding defeat. Then, slowly, he let her go and she rolled back up onto her feet.

She didn't take her eyes off the brothers. Flynn dared not move a muscle nor say a word. She turned to face them and a rumbling snarl came from deep within her. But it seemed to lack the fury of her earlier roars. It felt like a warning, rather than a sign she was about to attack. Flynn drew a sigh of relief.

Paddy then made a huge mistake. He simply turned to Flynn, smiled, and took a step towards him.

But, between them, and unnoticed by either of them, lay a thin crust of crumbling rock at the edge of the cliff. It collapsed under Paddy's weight. In an instant he was gone, tumbling off the edge of the cliff and plunging through the freezing air to the abyss below.

"PADDY!" screamed Flynn.

He threw himself onto his stomach to look over the edge, hoping that somehow his brother may have been able to grab something to stop his fall. To his horror, he saw his brother far below, tumbling over and over, plummeting towards the earth.

Something passed over Flynn's head. Springing like a tiger, Elton cleared the edge of the cliff with one leap. He spread his wings, gave two powerful flaps then folded them back against his body as he went into a high-speed dive after the boy.

Paddy was already halfway down the cliff face, dropping like a stone. But the green dragon chased him down like a bolt from a thundercloud.

Flynn watched in disbelief as Elton closed the gap on the falling boy. They were three quarters of the way down! But he saw the dragon stretch out a huge talon and grab his brother, the way an owl might pluck an insect out of the air.

By the time Elton managed to close his talon around Paddy, Flynn could see that they were close to the bottom of the cliff. Elton was still travelling in his dive and dropping at terrifying speed. Flynn watched as he spread his broad wings and tried to pull up and out of the dive, but the ground was coming horribly fast.

Flynn could see Elton's wings shaking terribly with the strain, and he saw that the dragon couldn't completely arrest his dive. He watched as Elton put three legs down to brace for the impact on the valley's rocky floor. He held his fourth leg close to his body, to protect the boy curled up in his talon. With a mighty roar which echoed back up the cliff face, Elton drew his wings down so hard Flynn thought they might snap.

It worked… almost. As the dragon levelled out, he still travelled at tremendous speed. Flynn saw his legs shudder as they hit the ground, absorbing the terrific impact. The dragon managed to leap back into the air, but he couldn't rise high enough to avoid a stand of young trees growing at the bottom of the valley. He barrelled into them, tucking into a tight, protective ball, with Paddy at his centre. The trees snapped like twigs and rocks and earth went flying before dragon and boy eventually came to a stop on the bank of the river.

Flynn peered over the edge, searching desperately for any signs of movement in the mess of shattered wood by the river's edge. As he watched, he suddenly felt a hot wind on his back. At the same time, he caught the scent of something pleasant but slightly burnt, like bread left cooking too long in the oven.

He rolled over and got quite a shock. The giant head of the female dragon hung directly over him. She, too, was looking at the devastation below.

Turning back, Flynn saw Elton uncurl his body on the forest floor to reveal Paddy. His brother looked like he was unconscious, lying unmoving in Elton's talon like a baby in a cot.

From high above, Flynn heard the *thud, thud, thud* of the helicopters. They were racing for the bottom of the canyon at terrific speed.

CHAPTER 16

Paddy slowly regained consciousness. It felt like he was swimming up to the surface from the depths of a dark lake. He was alive! He realised he must have passed out when Elton pulled up – the last thing he remembered was the incredible force with which he was pressed down into the dragon's talon as Elton tried to come out of his dive.

Paddy felt a hot breath. Opening his eyes, he looked up into the face of the green dragon. Elton was examining him, studying the boy with his huge, emerald green eyes. Paddy smiled at him, his nervousness now gone.

"Hello boy," he said. "We've named you Elton. How do you like it?"

The dragon snickered softly. A low rumble came from deep within the creature, like the purring of a gigantic cat.

Suddenly, Elton lifted his head and scanned the sky. Looking past him, Paddy saw what Elton had heard – the two helicopters were descending down towards them, fast.

"We need to go, Elton. Go!" he commanded. He rolled to his feet.

Paddy didn't hesitate. He clambered up onto Elton's back, trying to figure out where he might sit. There was no time to get comfortable. He sat astride the dragon's neck, wriggling up far enough to grab Elton's spines in both hands. Then, he hauled on them, hoping the dragon would respond.

Underneath him, Paddy felt Elton's muscles bunch, then uncoil as he sprang into the air, his mighty wings beating furiously. It was terrifying and terrific all at once, and he held on as tightly as he could, gripping the dragon's neck with his knees. Upwards they flew, circling around and around to gain height. He saw the helicopters immediately change course to give chase.

When Elton came level with the cliff top, there was Flynn, dwarfed by the giant female dragon standing behind him.

"Looks like you've made a new friend," yelled Paddy, smiling at his brother. "But I think we'd better go!"

The helicopters were coming fast. Paddy could see the co-pilots opening their doors and leaning out. They were connected to the machines by a harness, leaving their hands free to hold large and powerful rifles. Those rifles were now pointed at the brothers.

"Time to go," said Paddy. "Jump!"

Paddy could see Flynn was horrified at the thought of launching himself off the cliff, but there was nothing else for it. With his knees Paddy tried to guide Elton in the same way they did with Clappers, and the dragon seemed to understand.

He flew closer to the cliff edge.

Paddy watched Flynn take a few steps back to get a run up. Then, yelling in fear, he threw himself off the cliff, landing off-balance on Elton's broad back and scrambling to stay on. Paddy reached out an arm and managed to steady him, and Flynn clambered up to sit behind him, grabbing him around the waist. Paddy could feel his brother's hands trembling like crazy.

Behind them, the sound of the nearest helicopter was deafening. Paddy could feel the wind from its rotor blades.

"Hang on," he yelled as he felt Elton's wings tilt and draw in. Suddenly, they were once again in a dive, although this time Elton was in full control. Just as the dragon swooped, Paddy heard the loud crack of a rifle, but the tranquilliser dart flew harmlessly by.

Elton flew so close to the face of the cliff it made Paddy's hair stand on end, but he didn't try to adjust their course. He put his trust in Elton, and immediately realised what the dragon was doing. The helicopters couldn't fly as close to the rock as Elton could.

Just above the valley floor, Elton levelled out and streaked along the course of the river, flying low over the water. Behind them, the sound of the chasing helicopters became fainter as they dropped back, unable to keep up with the dragon through the tight turns of the canyon. Then they caught up again when Elton flew through open space.

Paddy felt Flynn urgently shaking his shoulder, and he turned to see a flash of movement to their left, between the trees. The female dragon was swooping and diving alongside them, keeping pace with Elton. It was marvellous to watch. It was even more exciting to actually be riding a dragon during this incredible acrobatic display.

The dragons were fresh and full of energy and flew fast. Before long, the sound of the helicopters became fainter and fainter. Finally, Paddy couldn't hear them at all. Elton banked hard, then swooped to land in under a tall tree, where they would be hidden from the helicopters above. The female landed seconds later. All four stood in silence, their chests heaving from the effort and excitement of the chase. They turned their eyes to the sky, searching for the helicopters.

The brothers listened for the next five minutes, until they were quite sure the helicopters had given up the chase. Finally, Paddy allowed himself to relax and properly acquaint himself with the beautiful green dragon which had now twice saved his life.

"Nice to meet you, Elton," said Paddy, scratching the giant creature under his chin. He seemed to like it.

"Careful," said Flynn, coming forward. But it was obvious that the dragon didn't mean to hurt them.

Elton suddenly lay down and rolled onto his back, his huge talons in the air. He puffed out a great cloud of smoke, and before it had cleared enough to see, whipped his tail around to trip over the brothers. They went tumbling onto the grass, laughing.

It then turned into a wrestling match, with Paddy and Flynn leaping onto Elton's belly. They were like ants on a cricket. Elton stood up quickly and sent them flying into the bushes without even meaning to. They whooped as they tried again and again, and Elton snorted and nodded his head with delight.

Elton's friend – the female dragon – watched with interest as they played, staying well off to one side.

"We'll have to give her a name, too," said Paddy.

"You're right," said Flynn. He looked thoughtful.

"How about Iris? She's yellow and blue, just like an iris flower."

Paddy nodded. "I like it. What do you think, Iris?"

The dragon looked at them without expression, which made the boys laugh.

"You'll get used to it," said Flynn. He walked over to the dragon. As he got closer, she shuffled uncomfortably, but held her ground. Flynn reached out his hand, palm down, and slowly he lowered it until he touched the top of Iris's nose.

"Her scales are so smooth!" he marvelled. "Iris – do you like your name?"

The dragon allowed him to gently stroke her nose and before long a deep rumble came from her throat. Paddy was learning that that was the sound of a happy dragon.

Suddenly, she pulled away and lifted her head high. She was listening to something. Then Paddy heard it too – the sound of the helicopters returning.

They shrank to the base of the tree and looked up through the branches. The noise grew louder and suddenly they flew directly overhead. They travelled at top speed, due west, in the direction of the brothers' house and the coast.

"Oh, no!" Paddy cried. His heart sank.

"Let them go, you bullies!" yelled Flynn.

Elton and Iris both let out terrific roars and raked the ground with their talons; they, too, had seen what the boys had seen. Two dragons, unconscious and bound up in heavy nets, swung from long ropes beneath the helicopters.

CHAPTER 17

When The Pitbull had seen the boys escaping on the back of the green dragon, he had to stop himself from smashing up both the screen he was watching as well as the fresh radio set.

But now that he had two dragons in his possession, he felt calmer. He knew that, eventually, he would succeed in this mission. He also knew that he would succeed in future missions that he was now planning. If he built a giant dragon enclosure, he would need many dragons to fill it.

Capturing the two dragons had been ridiculously easy. Once they lost sight of the boys and their dragons, The Pitbull had ordered the helicopters back up to the top of Mt Astonishing.

The co-pilots had done their work well, shooting a powerful tranquilliser dart at the first dragon they came across. The creatures actually seemed to be curious about these flying metal objects buzzing around them – they didn't become aggressive until the pilots fired at them. By then, it was too late. The tranquilliser worked quickly. Almost as soon as the dragons were hit, they became drowsy. Despite desperate attempts to stay in the air, the dragons couldn't help but spiral downwards, losing consciousness completely just moments after flopping clumsily in the snow.

Then it was a simple matter of firing a net out of the bottom of the helicopter. The Pitbull had ordered his engineers to design a special net cannon and it worked beautifully. As they rose, the net tightened and lifted the sleeping dragon with it.

The Pitbull heard the sound of the helicopters. Looking out of the bridge window, he could see them coming towards the ship, like two black dragonflies. Each had a bulging net strung beneath it. He hurried down the stairs to greet them on the deck. His men on the ship were already opening the cages in preparation for the beasts.

The dragons were incredibly heavy, but with the help of a small crane and ropes tied to the dragons' tails, they were dragged into the cages. The steel doors were secured with large bolts.

He had done it! He, The Pitbull, was now the proud owner of two enormous, ferocious dragons! He was the bravest of men!

He walked around the cages, examining the dragons. One of them was a bright pink with hundreds of deep green spines around its head and running the length of its back and tail. The other was as black as night all over, save for its blue eyes, which opened from time to time, then closed again under the influence of the tranquilliser.

The Pitbull stopped beside this dragon's head. It was just inches away through the bars of the cage. He was so close he could feel the heat of the creature's breath. Carefully, and very slowly, he put his hand through the bars and touched the nose of the dragon. There he kept it for a moment, enjoying the feeling of power. He was this huge creature's new master. From now on, he would decide what happened to this dragon. It would learn to understand that he was in command.

As these thoughts went through The Pitbull's head, he suddenly got the feeling he was being watched. He looked up. The black dragon's eye was open and staring at him. With enormous effort, the dragon bared its teeth, lifted its head, and let out a feeble roar.

It was all the drugged creature was able to do, but it gave The Pitbull quite a fright. Reeling backwards, he tripped on the edge of the cage's platform and fell, striking his head against the iron bars of the railings.

Pain seared through his skull. He let out an angry shout. His men came running. Embarrassed, he jumped to his feet. He looked around him and saw a toolbox that one of his men had carelessly left on deck. Reaching into it, he grabbed a handful of tools, and threw them at the black dragon with all his might. Then he turned, climbed the stairs, and strode back into the ship's bridge, slamming the door behind him.

From the far side of the deck, where she had been sitting against a lifeboat and looking out over the sea, Briar saw the whole thing.

CHAPTER 18

I t took Flynn and Paddy a long time to get Elton and Iris to calm down. The sight of their fellow dragons being captured by The Pitbull's helicopters had thrown them into a terrible rage. Elton was just about to take off in pursuit when Paddy and Flynn dived in front of him, grabbed hold of one of his legs and held on tight. They made reassuring noises to settle him. Flynn knew that if Elton chased the helicopters he would end up being captured too. He couldn't bear the thought of losing him so soon after they had found him.

Meanwhile, Iris vented her anger by setting several small trees ablaze with a long, fiery breath and ripping at the earth with her powerful talons.

When the dragons finally settled, the boys sat down underneath the tree to think.

"What are we going to do?" asked Paddy. "We can't just let The Pitbull take those poor dragons away from The Island!"

Flynn nodded. "You're right. We have to stop him, somehow."

"We don't even know where he is! And how long until those helicopters come back to capture more dragons?"

Flynn was silent, lost in thought and frustrated. He had no idea what to do.

"Let's take them on!" said Paddy angrily. "Let's see if Elton can pull those helicopters out of the sky!"

"That's crazy. What about those tranquilliser guns?" asked Flynn. "A huge dragon would be a hard thing to miss."

"Not if it's flying above the helicopter or on the opposite side from the man with the gun!" said Paddy.

Flynn shook his head.

"But Elton won't understand where to fly."

"Then we have to help him," said Paddy. "We have to guide him."

"I think you're forgetting something," said Flynn. "There are two helicopters."

Paddy smiled.

"There are two dragons. Only one of them we don't know how to fly… yet."

Flynn was dumbfounded.

"You mean… we fly on her as well?" He looked over at Iris, scratching her great trenches and snuffling through the ripped-up dirt. Her nose was covered in it.

Paddy nodded. Flynn could tell he was deadly serious. But they had no idea if Iris would even let them climb on her back.

"I bags Elton!" said Paddy, laughing and leaping to his feet.

Flynn smiled at his brother. "I thought you might say that."

Paddy looked at him, a serious expression on his face. "We don't have much time."

CHAPTER 19

Flynn could only just see Elton and Paddy, so high up they were little more than a black dot. Elton wheeled in a lazy circle, then suddenly flipped upside down and went into a speeding dive. Flynn heard his brother whoop with excitement. As they neared the ground, Elton spiralled through a corkscrew turn, pulled up and levelled out just a few feet above the ground. As they passed by, Flynn saw Paddy grin and wave madly at him.

Flynn could see that Paddy was a natural at flying a dragon. He was completely fearless and already able to control the direction and speed that Elton flew using just his knees.

Meanwhile, Flynn was stuck on the ground with Iris, who would only let him stroke her nose and nothing more. Five times now he had leapt upon her back and five times she had thrown him to the ground. She made little grunts and growls, but didn't seem angry. Instead, Flynn thought she seemed to be having fun, watching him sprawling in the dirt.

"That's enough!" he yelled at her. "You need to let me up. We need to fly together."

Iris looked at him quizzically and her head tilted over to one side like a puppy dog. A snicker came from her throat, which sounded to Flynn very like a laugh.

Flynn tried again, and once again had to pick himself up off the ground. He'd had enough. It was no use – he was getting nowhere.

He put his fingers to his mouth and gave a long, loud whistle to his brother. They would both have to fly on Elton's back and hope for the best.

High above, Paddy heard the faint sound of his brother's whistle. He looked down to see Flynn waving at him to come back. But then, suddenly, he heard another sound – a faint *thud, thud, thud*. Elton heard it too, and wheeled around. In the distance, moving past the snowy peaks of the Mystic Mountains, two black dots travelled at high speed. The helicopters were coming back!

Paddy pointed and shouted at the top of his lungs. He hoped Flynn could hear him. There was no time to pick up his brother – he and Elton would have to take on the helicopters alone.

He urged his dragon into a level, high-speed run directly at the helicopters. He didn't have a plan in mind, but he was angry, angrier than he'd ever been before. He let out a throaty howl at the helicopters. Elton roared with fury beneath him. Boy and beast were ready for a fight.

With Elton flying at top speed and the helicopters coming fast, they covered the distance between them in less than ten seconds. Suddenly, Elton and Paddy were locked in a furious, swirling dogfight with two dangerous metal machines.

Paddy knew that Elton wouldn't understand the danger of flying too close to the screaming blades of a helicopter. It was up to him to guide him away. Already, he could see that the two co-pilots had opened their doors and were now leaning out of the machines, aiming their tranquilliser guns at the twisting, turning dragon.

Paddy flew Elton straight at the helicopter, then pushed forward the dragon's spines to swoop under the skids and get to the side where the co-pilot couldn't shoot. But the other helicopter came around in a steep, banking turn and Paddy could see its co-pilot lining up to shoot. With lightning reactions, he flipped Elton onto his back and sent him into a dive. He heard a shot ring out, but Elton was moving like a jet fighter. The man missed.

"Woah! That was close," he said as he urged Elton down towards the canyon. Behind him, he heard the whining engines of the helicopters as they gave chase.

Elton could not shake the helicopters, no matter how skilfully he flew. The pilots were experts. Even if Paddy managed to lose one, the other would always be there, flying high above. They fired shot after shot. Each time they missed, but they were coming closer.

Beneath him, Paddy could sense Elton tiring. His turns were slowing and he didn't gain height as quickly. The helicopters were closing in.

Paddy and Elton reached the end of the canyon where the river fanned out into a series of braids that spread across the flat land. There was nowhere to hide. Desperately, he wheeled Elton around and started back up the canyon, at a loss for what else to do.

Elton bravely swooped and banked. He flew with every bit of speed he could muster. But it was no use.

The helicopters were now upon them. Paddy turned to see one of the men lining up his shot. He dug his right knee into Elton's neck, asking his brave dragon to wheel sharply once more. But he knew that it wouldn't be enough – that this time the dart would surely find its target.

He heard an angry roar over the terrific noise of the helicopter. It took him a moment to realise, however, that it hadn't come from Elton. Out of the corner of his eye, he saw a streaking blur of blue and yellow scorching past him at incredible speed. Was it the other helicopter? Elton was banking so hard that Paddy's vision blurred as they turned away. He heard the rifle's retort, but Elton didn't flinch. The man had missed!

Now, he heard another unfamiliar noise. It was the sound of the helicopter's engine, but it had changed. It strained and spluttered. As Elton straightened and Paddy's vision cleared, he looked up at the helicopter and got a shock. It was careening crazily across the sky, its rotors under full power, yet unable to halt its downward path. Beneath it, Iris clung to the skids. She flapped her wings at the speed of a hummingbird as she dragged down the helicopter with all her power. Clinging to Iris, completely upside down, was Flynn. Paddy whooped and punched the air.

Now the odds were even! But the fight wasn't over – not by a long way. Iris dropped from the helicopter and the machine tore back up into the sky under full power. It banked sharply and came back for another attack. The Pitbull's pilots knew that Elton was tiring. They could also see, as Paddy could, that Flynn had little control over his dragon – he could barely stay on her back!

Paddy looked at his brother and marvelled at his bravery. It was obvious that Iris didn't understand Flynn's commands. He could see his brother battling to stay in control. Yet still he had come to his rescue.

It was clear to Paddy that their best chance was to split up, so he turned Elton away and steered him towards the mountain. One helicopter gave chase, while the other sped after Flynn and Iris.

CHAPTER 20

Flynn was freaking out.

When he had heard the sound of the
helicopters returning he didn't stop to think.
He simply ran at Iris, leapt upon her back and
grabbed hold of the spines around her head.
The only reason she hadn't thrown him off was
because she was too busy looking at the helicopters,
and at Elton.

Now he was in the most impossibly dangerous
situation of his life. He was hundreds of feet in
the air, trying with all his might to hang onto a

powerful dragon. She flew completely upside down or cartwheeled through the sky in the most extraordinary way. Flynn wasn't sure if Iris was even aware that he was on her back. She flew where she wanted, despite him using his knees and pulling on her spines to guide her. It was clear that he was only along for the ride.

Iris flew at the helicopters and then turned away so hard it made Flynn's head spin. At one point he almost blacked out. He flattened himself against her neck and held on as tightly as he could. Iris roared and sent fireballs at the helicopter, but they had little effect. The man simply pulled his door over, using it as a shield. He then opened it again after the fireball had passed. The Pitbull had prepared his aircraft for this purpose and they weren't affected at all by fire.

As Iris came around for another charge at the helicopter, Flynn saw the gunman casually swing out of the cockpit. He raised his gun and waited. Flynn dug his knees into Iris, first one side, then the other, but she didn't respond. Instead, she flew straight towards the helicopter in a fury. She was going to attack it head-on.

Iris let forth a furious roar as she approached. She raised her talons up before her like an eagle about to strike its prey. It was the moment the gunman had been waiting for. Her stomach was exposed. He shot his tranquilliser dart into her as easily as he might into the side of a barn. At the same time, the pilot opened the throttle and the helicopter shot upwards, out of harm's way.

Iris flew harmlessly beneath the helicopter. Flynn felt her shudder. Her wings twitched and faltered as the strong tranquilliser drug quickly took effect. Bravely, she wheeled and spat a feeble fireball at the helicopter, which simply hovered. Flynn could see the men smiling in the cockpit as Iris began to lose height. He gritted his teeth in anger and fear. He could do nothing but hold on and hope.

Iris battled the drug for a long time, flapping hard and trying again and again to attack the helicopter. But, eventually, she lost the battle.

She was losing consciousness. She went into a long, downward glide towards the forest. Lower and lower they flew, until they were just a few feet from the tree tops. Flynn braced for the impact. He was afraid that at this speed both he and Iris would be killed.

Suddenly, there were no trees beneath them! They had flown over a small clearing. Flynn thought they might just have a chance. Though she could barely keep her eyes open, Iris turned for the flattest part of the ground. She was close to blacking out. The ground loomed. But they had travelled too far across the clearing! They were approaching the other side, where they would surely strike the solid trunks of the trees and be killed!

Just as she was about to pass out, Iris extended her talons. They struck the ground and dragged through the earth. Finally, her head dipped and she spun forward, rolling end over end. Flynn was violently thrown off and he tumbled like a rag doll. He passed between two trees on the edge of the clearing and flew headlong into the forest, his head striking a log with terrible force. Groggily, he looked up, back out to the clearing. He saw Iris, lying at the end of a long trench of broken earth and uprooted shrubs. She wasn't moving. Then, his mind clouded and everything went black.

CHAPTER 21

This time, Paddy had a plan.

He and Elton had seen Iris dragging down the helicopter. Paddy realised it was probably the best way to win this battle without Elton being shot with a tranquilliser dart. Unfortunately, it seemed the pilot had also figured this out. He was using all his skill to stay level with the dragon.

It was going to require Elton to find reserves of strength that Paddy didn't know if he had left. The dragon had been flying as fast as he could for almost thirty minutes. Paddy had no idea if he could keep it up.

Up ahead, Paddy spotted a ridge line extending halfway up the side of Mt Astonishing. He knew that on the other side was a sheer drop, a cliff that fell almost half a mile to the valley floor. Paddy leaned forward to let Elton know he wanted him to fly as fast as possible. Beneath him, he felt the dragon's muscles straining as Elton flapped his wings powerfully, catapulting them through the air at high speed.

Elton's efforts had put some distance on the helicopter. As they flew over the ridge, Paddy directed Elton down, wheeling him around hard to come back to the cliff face. Elton grabbed hold of the rock with his powerful talons, clinging on like a bat to the wall of a cave. They were hidden from the approaching helicopter. Paddy could feel the dragon sucking in huge lungfuls of air as he struggled to catch his breath.

Elton had less than ten seconds to recover. Paddy hoped it was enough for one final effort.

As the helicopter crested the ridge line, he gripped Elton tightly and the dragon sprang up, flapping furiously. When the helicopter passed overhead, Elton turned upside down and closed his talons on the skids. The wrench was terrific and Paddy almost fell. His legs slipped off and he hung from Elton's neck, his feet dangling over half a mile of thin air.

At first, the helicopter appeared to be winning the battle as it roared upwards, pulling dragon and boy back over the ridge line and down towards the forest. At least there wouldn't be quite so far to fall, thought Paddy, although he knew that even at this height he would never survive.

Then, Elton cleverly began to use the helicopter's power against it. Instead of trying to wrestle the helicopter down towards the ground, Elton pushed its skids up and out to one side. The helicopter tilted crazily and Paddy heard the pilot shouting in panic. Now that it was on its side, it was flying sideways too. When Elton pushed a little more, the helicopter tilted further, almost upside down. They plummeted towards the ground. The gunman flew back inside his cockpit, slamming into the pilot, who fought to maintain control. Now Paddy was more or less upright and able to clamber back onto the dragon's neck.

Elton dragged the helicopter first one way and then the other. It crabbed madly across the sky. Paddy was amazed to see the co-pilot swing right out of the cockpit and dangle at the end of his harness rope. In his fright, he dropped his gun, which fell harmlessly to the mountainside, disappearing into the thick trees far below.

Quickly the helicopter lost height. Its engine rose to a high-pitched whine as the pilot battled the dragon. Lower and lower they flew, until Paddy was sure he and Elton had won the fight. As they descended, the rotor blades began to slice through the tree tops. Paddy saw bits of tree and blade break off and spin away into the forest. It was time to get out of there. He twisted his knees and leaned back. The dragon kicked powerfully, sending the helicopter careening into the trees, where its rotor blades made an awful noise as they flew to bits against the thick branches.

Free of the helicopter, Elton flapped hard, rising above the trees. Paddy saw the helicopter plunge down through the canopy. It bounced from branch to branch, eventually crunching to the ground in a tangle of twisted metal and broken timber. While Elton circled, Paddy saw the two men stagger out of the mangled machine and run away into the forest.

From further down the valley came a deep rumble, like thunder. The sound echoed against the cliffs, then died away. A moment later Paddy heard another sound: the *thud, thud, thud* of the other helicopter.

CHAPTER 22

From the air Paddy saw the clearing and the broad scar of rocks and earth where Iris had obviously crashed and skidded across the ground. But, as he and Elton approached, the other helicopter lifted off from the clearing, with Iris dangling beneath it. Elton let out a pained bellow, and Paddy knew he wanted to give chase, but his dragon couldn't stay in the air another minute.

And Paddy must find his brother.

Elton roared with frustration and landed in the clearing. Leaping off his back, Paddy sprinted to the

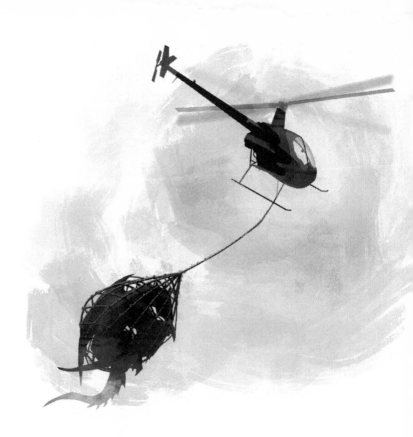

end of the trench that Iris had made. His heart sank.

Flynn was nowhere to be seen. Perhaps he had

been scooped up in the net too!

"Flynn!" Paddy yelled at the top of his lungs.
Had he run away?

Then, from somewhere in the trees Paddy heard
a faint groan. He sprinted into the forest, charging

through the thick undergrowth. He almost tripped

over a log, but looking down saw that it was

his brother!

Flynn gazed up at him. He looked confused. Blood

was matting in his hair and running down his cheek.

"Paddy," he croaked, holding out his hand.

He tried to get up, but he got no further than his

knees when his eyes glazed over and he collapsed

onto the ground.

CHAPTER 23

Flynn awoke to the sensation of water running over his face. As he slowly came to, he looked up into his brother's eyes, staring at him with concern. Paddy was cleaning the mud and blood from Flynn's cheek.

"Ouch," said Flynn.

"You and Iris could have done with a little more practice," replied Paddy with a grin. "That was some of the worst flying I've ever seen. Here, take a drink."

Flynn drank deeply from the flask Paddy held to his lips. He could feel the cool mountain water quickly reviving him. He sat up.

"Are you hurt?" asked Paddy.

Flynn felt himself all over. Apart from some nasty bruises and scrapes, nothing appeared to be damaged. He was still a little woozy.

"I'm OK. How long was I out? Where are we?"

All around them was thick forest. A short distance away, he could see Elton lying under a tree. His giant chest rose and fell – he was fast asleep.

Paddy put a finger to his lips.

"Elton's exhausted," he said. "Let's leave him for a little while and go check out the helicopter he brought down."

Flynn's eyes widened. "He did it?" he asked.

Paddy nodded. A smile lit up his face.

"Elton was awesome," he said.

As the boys walked quietly through the forest, Lightning fluttered down from the trees and sat on

Flynn's shoulder. He stared at the cut on Flynn's head and made a gentle snickering sound.

"Where have you been?" asked Flynn. He remembered that Lightning had flown away in fright as soon as the helicopters arrived. As Flynn spoke, he noticed a tiny rolled up piece of paper attached to the bird's leg.

"Paddy! Look!"

Carefully, he unrolled the message and flattened it on his knee. He immediately recognised his mother's handwriting. He read aloud:

Dear Flynn and Paddy,

We hope that because Lightning is still free, that means you are, too.

You must know by now that we are imprisoned in our home and that seven men are here. Two are inside and the other five are surrounding the house with guns.

We think that The Pitbull is on a ship anchored somewhere off the coast of The Island. It takes a helicopter about five minutes to fly from the ship to our house so it can't be too far away – in a westerly direction.

We are so very worried, but we are unhurt and in good spirits.

Please be careful and stay away from the house until this is all over. When The Pitbull gets what he wants he will surely leave and take his men with him.

We love you so much.

Mum, Dad, and Ada

Flynn and Paddy read the note in silence. Anger rose up inside Flynn like water boiling in a kettle. It only strengthened his determination.

"We must be somewhere close to the crashed helicopter now," said Paddy, peering through the trees.

Flynn flicked Lightning up into the air and gave three short whistles – the sign for the falcon to hunt. Soon they heard the familiar *"squee"*, and before long they were standing in front of the tangled wreckage of the crashed helicopter. The men were long gone, probably on their way back to the brothers' house. That made a total of nine men guarding their parents and sister. Flynn pushed it out of his mind.

There was little of interest in the helicopter – just some chocolate wrappers and discarded coffee cups.

As the boys stood silently in the darkening forest – the sun had lowered to the horizon – Flynn realised how hopeless their situation was. However, there was one thing he was sure of. He knew that they weren't about to give up. Not now.

CHAPTER 24

The sight of his helicopter flying across the water, the setting sun behind it, and an unconscious dragon dangling beneath, was just as good the second time around.

The Pitbull was so close to success he could almost taste it! Three down, one to go!

As the helicopter dropped its cargo on the deck, The Pitbull stepped out of the bridge for a closer look. His breathing quickened. This was a trophy specimen – larger than the other two dragons and far more impressive. In the setting sun, its wings were the colour of a gold bar. He felt the ship list slightly to one side under its terrific weight.

As his men hauled the magnificent creature into its cage and clanged home the iron bolt, The Pitbull cracked his knuckles and smiled. Almost done.

He scanned the horizon for the other helicopter. Any second now, it would appear, bringing the final dragon. They could then up-anchor, fire up the engines and be home by lunchtime tomorrow.

But the helicopter was nowhere to be seen. He listened. Nothing. He waited ten long minutes on deck before growing impatient and going back up to the bridge. He tried to activate the radio and video camera, but it was just a confusing array of lights and buttons. He hadn't a clue how to operate it. As he jabbed and prodded, a gnawing feeling grew in the pit of his stomach – surely those rats of brothers hadn't been able to stop a helicopter?

"Briar!" he roared. "Get here, now! Make this camera work! Briar! Briar! Where are you? Where the hell is EVERYBODY?"

The captain of the ship came running to help.

"Connect me to the helicopter – now!" yelled The Pitbull. "Briar! Where is she?"

The captain stammered. "Yes, sir. No, sir. I mean, I don't know where she is, sir. Shall I go and find her, sir?"

The captain began hurrying away.

"WHERE ARE YOU GOING?!" screamed The Pitbull. "GET BACK HERE! CONNECT ME TO MY PILOTS, YOU IDIOT!"

The captain scrambled back to the controls in a panic. He twisted the dials and with great relief he saw that he had been successful in connecting to Air Pitbull One.

"GET BACK!" yelled The Pitbull. "GET OUT OF MY WAY!"

CHAPTER 25

As the boys turned away from the ruined helicopter and began the short walk back to where Elton was sleeping, Paddy heard a faint crackle.

He stopped.

"Did you hear something?"

There was another crackle, like an egg being fried on a hot pan, then a loud beep. They heard the fuzz of static. It was coming from the helicopter!

The two boys jogged back. They poked their heads inside the cockpit.

"It's probably just the sound a dying helicopter makes," Paddy said with a grin.

But the screen on the control panel appeared to have a faint glow. Then, it started to flicker – green, then blue. Slowly, as they watched, a shape appeared, first on one side of the screen, then the other. Soon they could see it was a man, walking to and fro. Then the brothers could plainly tell who it was. They were looking at The Pitbull.

You can use the **AR Reads** app on your device to view this video. Simply start up the app, then point the device at this page and meet The Pitbull in person. Be warned – he has an awful plan! If you don't have a device – don't worry – just read on!

At first, the boys were confused. The Pitbull was ranting about someone named Briar, who he ordered to be found and locked in the engine room for the night without food, blankets, or even light!

Then, they watched with some amusement as The Pitbull realised he wasn't looking at his pilots, but two young boys. Bewilderment showed on his face, which soon turned to anger as he realised that his helicopter and pilots were lost.

They tried to speak to The Pitbull. Paddy, in particular, had some things he wanted to say. But, it seemed that the microphone had been damaged in the crash. However, the brothers clearly heard what The Pitbull was saying.

He ran through his usual list of insults, but then his expression changed. He smiled. It sent a shiver down Paddy's spine. It was clear that The Pitbull had an idea.

"I'm so glad we've had this chance to catch up," he said. "Here's why: I have heavily armed, well-trained men guarding your family. All I have to do is make one call and you will never see them again."

Paddy understood The Pitbull's plan even before he finished explaining it. He wanted the brothers to deliver Elton to him, or else their mother, father, and sister would be harmed or imprisoned. The Pitbull gave them the location of his ship – ten miles due west of the island – and told them they had just one hour to deliver the dragon.

"Better hurry," said The Pitbull, smiling.

A terrible, overwhelming sadness struck Paddy. He looked at his brother, and could tell he felt the same. But they had no choice.

Flynn and Paddy turned and ran.

They yelled to rouse Elton from his sleep. To their relief, when they reached him he was wide awake and alert.

The brothers flung themselves onto his back. He seemed to understand that they were in a desperate hurry. He immediately leapt into the air, beating his wings so hard and climbing so fast the boys had to hold on for dear life.

As they cleared the tree tops, Paddy turned Elton for the coast. He leaned forward and Elton responded with a burst of speed. Soon, the ground beneath them was a blur.

Paddy yelled above the rushing wind.

"How long do you think it will take for us to get there?"

Flynn shrugged.

"Perhaps ten minutes – if we can find it straight away. It's almost dark."

Already, they had passed over the Paradise Peninsula and were racing out over the open sea. Beyond the foaming white of the breakers on the reef, the ocean was a deep, forbidding black. Paddy urged the dragon upward, so that they could see further in all directions.

"Do you believe him?"

Paddy had been turning the question over in his mind. Would The Pitbull really free them and their family after they delivered Elton to him? In his heart, he knew the answer.

As their brave dragon flew further out across the dark sea, unaware that the brothers were delivering him into captivity for the rest of his life, Paddy felt increasingly afraid and powerless.

Then, suddenly, far below them, he saw it – The Pitbull's ship. Its powerful spotlights shone brightly up into the sky – they were searching for the arriving dragon. As they came closer, Paddy could make out the figures of several gunmen on the deck of the ship, ready to shoot tranquilliser darts into Elton as soon as he landed and probably into him, too!

Paddy guided Elton down towards the ship. He squeezed the tears from his eyes.

Suddenly, he felt Flynn grip him tightly.

"Pull up. Turn around," said Flynn.

Paddy needed no further encouragement. He turned Elton away immediately. He guided him into a high, slow spiral as the brothers talked.

"I have an idea," said Flynn.

"About time," replied Paddy. He grinned. He knew Flynn would think of something.

As the brothers circled above the ship, Paddy's heart began to race as he listened carefully to the plan his brother had come up with.

When he had finished, Paddy whistled.

"That's crazy. Let's do it."

CHAPTER 26

Half an hour had passed since the boys had watched The Pitbull's chilling message. There was no time to lose!

Paddy turned his head and yelled to his brother above the rushing wind.

"Remember when you bellyflopped off the cliff? Well, this is going to be a lot worse!"

He brought Elton out of a long dive to level off at high speed, just a few feet above the churning waves. They were five hundred yards from the ship and closing fast.

"Yeah – thanks a lot," yelled Flynn in reply.

Sea spray, whipped up by the wind and swell, stung Flynn's face. Elton was hurtling directly for the bow of the ship. Its powerful spotlights created a tower of bright light rising from its deck, up into the sky.

Now they were closer, Flynn could see the gunmen on deck. As he hoped, the men were all looking up, waiting for the dragon to appear.

He scrambled to his feet and hung on to Paddy's shoulders. His brother adjusted Elton's course slightly, now aiming for just in front of the bow of the ship – between the overhanging steel hull and the anchor rope disappearing down into the water. It would be their best chance at going unnoticed. The speed they were travelling at was terrific, but they daren't slow down in case one of the men happened to look down and see them.

"Good luck," he heard Paddy say over the wind. He gave his brother's shoulders a squeeze in reply.

As they passed under the huge prow of the ship, Elton folded his wings back against his body to rocket through the narrow triangle space created by the ship's bow and the anchor rope. At the same time, Flynn simply stepped off the speeding dragon and braced for the impact.

CHAPTER 27

"**D**amn it. Looks like we're going to be staying the night."

"Maybe not. The boss said to be ready for an important communication at exactly 7.30pm – that's only fifteen minutes away. It might be the order to pull out and go home."

"Let's hope so. I've had enough of babysitting this lot."

In the still night air, everything the men were saying inside could clearly be heard through the open window. Paddy lay in the thick bushes near his house. He had left Elton well away, deep in the forest. He'd almost yelled out in fright when Clappers came trotting out of the trees, closely followed by Coco. They had skittered nervously when they saw Elton, but Paddy coaxed them forward and before long they were sniffing the giant dragon with interest.

Paddy had ordered them all to stay put and then quickly made his way to the house, trying to run as silently as possible and stay in the darkest shadows. There wasn't enough time to be careful.

He knew what he had to do, but had absolutely no idea how to do it.

The men were still at their stations surrounding the house, but Paddy noticed they weren't exactly on high alert. The guard directly below the window was lying on his back, his head resting on his pack. His eyes were closed and he appeared to be sound asleep. Another guard, on the other side of the house, smoked a cigarette and idly twirled his pistol on his trigger finger. They were clearly bored.

Paddy estimated that he had less than ten minutes before The Pitbull's hour was up. As he sat in silence, watching the sleeping guard, he suddenly had an idea.

He quietly rose and jogged back into the darkness of the forest. Then, he paid a visit to his father's shed, where he grabbed a large coil of rope. Outside, lying in the grass, he noticed a large, dark shape. It was one of the huge nets the helicopters used to catch the dragons. It must be a spare.

Then Paddy made his way back to Clappers, who was contentedly chewing a mouthful of grass.

"I need you, girl," said Paddy. "Are you ready?"

The horse responded with a quiet whinny.

Taking one end of the rope, Paddy fashioned a type of harness and placed it around Clappers' neck. Then, careful to be as quiet as possible, he guided her back to the house.

CHAPTER 28

Flynn held onto the anchor rope, wincing in pain. He'd been here for ten minutes already. Time was running out, but he was still too winded and sore to climb it.

When Flynn had hit the water it knocked every bit of breath out of him. And, unfortunately, breath was just what he needed. The force of the impact and the angle that he struck forced him down, deep beneath the surface.

He could only imagine the noise and the splash that he made when he had hit. He knew it was important to stay under the water for as long as he could. But his lungs screamed for air.

Flynn had turned on his back, and looked up at the ship. He could just make out its outline against the bright glare of the spotlights. Two dark shapes interrupted the curved line of the hull – guards peering over the railing! They must have heard the splash and rushed to investigate.

Flynn had fought the urge to strike out for the surface, despite how badly he needed to take a breath. To his enormous relief the guards had disappeared, and Flynn finally came up and took the deepest, sweetest gulp of air he had ever taken.

But now, time was up. He must attempt the anchor rope. It looked impossibly high; Flynn had no idea if he even had the strength to climb it.

CHAPTER 29

P addy had never been more frightened in his life. The closer he got to the guard, the more he realised what a crazy plan this was. But he was out of time. And now he had no choice.

Closer and closer he crawled to the sleeping man. He moved just one leg or one arm at a time, placing it carefully, trying to avoid dry leaves or twigs – anything that might make a noise. He was just a few feet away.

At the side of the house, in the gloom, Paddy could just make out the tall figure of another of the guards. He was standing to attention, but thankfully he was facing in the opposite direction.

If that guard happened to turn his way, or the sleeping guard woke up, it would all be over.

Paddy crossed the last few inches with infinite care. Then, slowly, quietly, he extended his arm, holding out the noose he had made in the other end of the rope. As softly as he could, he lowered the noose over the guard's outstretched foot.

The man stirred and mumbled something aloud. Paddy's breath caught in his throat. A few terrible seconds passed before Paddy heard the guard's breathing deepen again.

He could bear it no longer. Paddy leapt to his feet, turned, and sprinted into the forest, yelling loudly for Clappers. He gave her a sharp slap on the rump. She took off like a runaway train.

The coils of rope whipped out at a terrific rate as Clappers bolted into the darkness. Then suddenly it jerked straight, tightening the noose around the guard's foot. Paddy heard his panicked screams as he was dragged after the horse.

CHAPTER 30

Flynn's arms burned with the effort of climbing the anchor rope. It was thicker than his arm and slick with seaweed and slime. He needed all the strength of his legs to grip the rope. Desperately, he hauled himself, hand over hand, towards the gap in the deck railing.

He finally made it, grabbing the solid steel of the hull with relief. But, he had no idea what he would find when he pulled himself up over the side. Would there be anywhere to hide? Would the men see him straightaway? He didn't have

enough strength left to take a quick look and assess his options.

He simply pulled himself up with a final, painful effort and slid onto his back on the deck, exhausted.

It was only sheer luck that the gunmen didn't see him. They were all looking up into the sky, half-blinded by the powerful lights. He scrambled to the anchor winch and pressed himself into its shadow. Peeping around the side, he saw the remaining helicopter perched on the deck like a giant black insect. Beyond that were four enormous steel cages, three of which now housed a dragon. The poor creatures sat quite still, even though the tranquillisers must have worn off. Their spirits were already broken.

He wanted to scream and attack anyone who stood in his way. But he knew it wouldn't be any use. He would be caught straightaway. He realised that he was trapped. He couldn't move in any direction without being seen by one of the gunmen.

Flying proudly over the deck on a tall flagpole, a black flag with the white dog's head insignia whipped to and fro in the freshening easterly. A storm was brewing, and it gave him an idea. He pulled out his knife and began to saw through the anchor rope.

CHAPTER 31

As the guard came speeding past him, slithering over the leaf litter of the forest, Paddy saw the terrified look on his face. He couldn't help but giggle.

"Wakey wakey," he said to the man as he rocketed by.

Then, as quickly and quietly as he could, Paddy doubled back to the big tree and climbed up through its branches so he could see in the window.

As he suspected, all hell had broken loose! Men ran in all directions around the house, shouting at the

top of their lungs. There was little organisation.
The men simply gathered at the side of the
house where the guard had disappeared,
then blindly ran into the forest, following his
distant screams.

It was the chance Paddy had been waiting
for. Deftly, he swung down out of the tree and
landed lightly on the windowsill. He was inside in
seconds, crouched down behind the radio unit.
It was a tangled mess of coloured wires. He had
absolutely no idea what he was doing, but it
didn't much matter. He only had to make sure it
was destroyed. He began to pull out the wires,
ripping them from the back and stuffing them into
his pockets.

Paddy thought about charging down the
hallway and freeing his parents and sister, but
already he could hear some of the men returning.
Just before he climbed back out of the window, he
noticed two mobile phones on the table. Grabbing

them, he flung them out of the window into the dark forest.

With a leap Paddy was back in the tree. Quickly, he climbed down. Walking a wide semi-circle around the guards, he began to make his way back to where he left Elton. On the way, he met Clappers, who still wore the rope harness. At some point during her bolt through the forest, the rope had snapped, and the man was now nowhere to be seen.

"Where's your new friend?" he asked her, smiling. "I bet he has a heck of a sore bottom."

Clappers could see in the dark better than Paddy and she guided him back to Elton.

As they neared, Paddy heard Coco give a low, threatening growl. It was followed by a frightened whimper. Emerging into the moonlight, Paddy grinned. The man who had been dragged behind Clappers now cowered under the fierce guard of Elton and Coco. He was a curled into a tight ball on the ground, frightened out of his wits.

Immediately, it gave Paddy an idea.

"If I was you, I wouldn't move a muscle," he said to the man. "One word from me and that dragon will eat you alive."

CHAPTER 32

Time was up. There was no doubt about it. Flynn didn't have a watch, but he was certain more than an hour had passed since the brothers had watched The Pitbull's awful message. He prayed Paddy had been successful.

Flynn was still trapped, hunkered down behind the winch. The anchor rope was cut through and he'd dropped it off the side where it disappeared under the waves. They were now adrift in a strong wind rising from the east. His wet clothes were chilling him to the bone.

The Pitbull had walked up and down the stairs to the bridge several times. When he was inside, Flynn couldn't hear what he was saying, but he could see him through the window, yelling and waving his arms. At one point, Flynn saw him lift a black box high above his head. Colourful wires were ripped from the wall. The Pitbull then kicked open the bridge door, hurried down the stairs and walked across the deck. Coming to the railing, screaming with rage, he hurled the radio overboard. He stalked angrily back inside. His men ran everywhere, trying to satisfy their master.

Eventually, The Pitbull ordered the spotlights to be shut off. He bellowed at the guards to get out of his sight. Then, Flynn heard him order the helicopter pilot to be ready to leave in half an hour. With that, The Pitbull disappeared through the steel door that led below deck, heading for his quarters.

For ten agonising minutes, Flynn watched as the helicopter pilot filled his machine with fuel. Then, thankfully, he too disappeared below deck.

It was the chance Flynn had been waiting for. Keeping low, he ran straight for the helicopter. Flynn was certain of one thing: he mustn't let it take off, or he may never see his family again.

Pulling out his knife, Flynn went to work on the helicopter. He unscrewed a panel and cut through all the pipes and cables inside it. Strange coloured fluids leaked out and ran down the side of the fuselage. He checked the door – it was open! Quickly he jumped into the cockpit and stabbed at all the delicate parts of the control panel. He levered off buttons and pulled the needles from gauges. With the butt of his knife, he smashed any screen that he saw.

He hoped it was enough! Leaping out, he sprinted across the deck, raced up the stairs to the bridge, and went inside.

The main lights were turned off, but Flynn was able to see by the glow coming from the various screens of the ship's control panel. He considered smashing up the controls, but realised it would probably make too much noise.

Turning to leave, something caught Flynn's eye. On the table, in the middle of the bridge, was a sheaf of papers. The top sheet showed a picture of the ship from above. On the bottom of the page was a small picture of a phone, just like the ones in his rucksack. Hurriedly he pulled one out. The waxed cloth had kept it perfectly dry.

Flynn tapped at the bottom of the screen. It lit up. Could it work? He searched for the icon with the letters AR and pressed it. Then, he held the phone over the picture and waited for something to happen.

Use the **AR Reads** app on your device to see the layout of The Pitbull's ship, and see where Flynn might decide to go next. Point the device at this page and see for yourself! If you don't have a device – don't worry – just keep reading!

When the 3D image of the ship appeared on the screen of the phone, Flynn gasped. He could see the layout of the vessel – the sleeping quarters, galley, dining room, and the engine room were all clearly marked.

He quickly committed it to memory, then shut down the phone and stuffed it into his rucksack. He went back out on deck, careful to make sure there were no guards. He had seen the door through which The Pitbull had gone, and now he quietly entered it and went below deck.

CHAPTER 33

Paddy was beginning to enjoy himself.

So far, he had two guards tied up and sitting quietly under the watchful eyes of Elton and Coco – the man whom Clappers had dragged away from the house, and another guard sent to look for him. The second man had stumbled out of the forest, taken one look at Elton and dropped his gun in fright, begging for mercy.

Now Coco prowled back and forth in front of the captives, growling like a tiger. The men were silent, staring at the ground.

Paddy figured he now had enough to bargain with.

Leaving Coco to guard the men, he leapt on Elton's back and they took off into the dark sky, turning once again for the house. Paddy peered down into the darkness and circled high above, until finally he made out the tiny roof of his father's shed. Slowly, Paddy guided Elton down, peering carefully into the dark to ensure there were no guards. Finally they glided in, landing softly on the grass.

Paddy smiled. There, still sitting beside the shed, was the spare dragon net.

CHAPTER 34

Down below deck, Flynn heard the sound of guards talking, but it was difficult to tell from which direction it came. Already, the details of the ship's layout weren't making sense and he only had a rough idea of where he was going.

He tiptoed down the long hallways, stopping every now and again to listen. He knew he had to find another stairwell, to take him deeper into the ship. It wasn't where he remembered on the 3D model. At one point, from behind a door, he thought he heard the clucking of chickens and the bleat of a goat.

Suddenly, in front of him, a door swung open!

Light spilled into the hallway. Flynn quickly shrank back into the recess of another doorway, praying that it wouldn't open, too.

Then, he heard The Pitbull's voice. He was ranting and raving, apparently to himself. He was coming towards him! Flynn dropped to the floor and curled into a ball in the shadows. It was a terrible hiding place, but there was nowhere else to go. It felt like his heart might beat right out of his chest. The Pitbull would surely see him!

But The Pitbull was so deeply absorbed in his conversation with himself that he walked right by the doorway without so much as a sideways glance. Slung over his shoulder, he carried an arsenal of guns.

Flynn heaved a sigh of relief. He willed his hands to stop shaking. He felt like he was going to vomit.

When the Pitbull was gone, Flynn continued along the hallway. There, stencilled in black paint on the steel door at the end, was the sign he was looking for: 'Engine Room'. He slid back the lock and entered, closing the door behind him.

CHAPTER 35

"Time to go home, boys!" yelled Paddy. One by one, the guards came running, either from inside the house or from their stations around it. With great satisfaction Paddy noticed the looks of horror on their faces.

Paddy and Elton hovered directly above them. Elton's wings beat strongly, rising dust and leaves off the ground. He roared at them, and crackling sparks flew out of his mouth. Paddy leaned over and took aim with his bow.

The men finally came to their senses and lifted their guns.

"Do that and the dragon drops the net!" shouted Paddy.

Paddy saw the guards peer into the darkness. Dangling from Elton's talon was the huge dragon net. And inside it were the guards' two missing colleagues.

"Do what he says!" whimpered one of the captured men, clearly terrified that Elton would let them go.

"Put the guns down and stand together," instructed Paddy.

The seven men had no choice. They dropped their guns and gathered into a nervous group.

Slowly, Paddy guided Elton down, until the net just touched the ground beside them.

"Now, climb into the net," ordered Paddy. He kept his arrow pulled back to his cheek and aimed directly at the leader.

Two of the men hesitated and Paddy gave Elton a tap with his heels. The dragon responded by launching a fireball. It hit the ground beside the men, sending them sprawling and screaming in terror, flames licking at their clothes. The terrific heat singed their hair and eyebrows. It was enough to put any thoughts of fighting, or running away, out of their minds. One by one, they obediently climbed into the net.

Paddy leaned forward and whispered into Elton's ear.

"Let's go!"

With a bellow, Elton powered up into the dark sky. Below, nine men struggled in the hanging net, like fish behind a trawler. The weight was terrific and it took all of Elton's strength to lift them into the sky.

As Paddy looked down at his house, he caught sight of his sister. Ada was waving up at him from the window of the bedroom. He smiled and waved back, hoping she could see him in the darkness.

CHAPTER 36

The engine room of The Pitbull's ship was completely dark. Flynn stumbled down a short ladder, running his hands over the walls, feeling for a light switch, but could find none.

It was hopeless. It was too dark to see anything. Flynn was ready to give up when he thought of the phones in his rucksack.

Quickly he pulled one out and tapped at the bottom of the screen. It lit up, and in the faint glow, he could see the ship's two huge engines side by side in the centre of the room. A bewildering array of pipes, gaskets, valves and gauges came out of them.

Flynn walked over to a workbench. It was neatly organised with rows of bottles and tubes. They had labels such as grease, oil, solvents – Flynn didn't know what any of them were.

Above it, on the wall, tools were arranged on wall hooks – screwdrivers, wrenches, saws, hammers and pull-out drawers of nuts and bolts – some as big as Flynn's hand, others no larger than a pin head.

Flynn placed the phone on the bench. Its blue glow cast an eerie light across the room. He picked up a hammer with one hand and a hacksaw with the other. Then, turning back to the diesel engines, he went to work. He used the hammer to bust open valves and smash the glass of the gauges. He sawed through pipes and bent over levers. It made a terrible noise. But Flynn didn't care any more – all his anger at The Pitbull he now directed into destroying the ship's engines.

As Flynn sent a gauge flying across the room, he noticed the large steel caps atop each engine. It took all of his strength to unscrew them. He peered down into the dark holes, but there was nothing in there to break.

He knew he hadn't done enough. The ship's engineers would easily be able to fix the small amount of damage he had caused. It was hopeless. He sank to the ground in despair, his back against an engine.

Outside, he heard muffled shouting and footsteps. They must have discovered the damage to the helicopter and were now searching the ship for him. It was over.

Sitting there in the engine room, Flynn thought of his parents, his brother, and his sweet little sister. He may never see them again. He thought of his grandparents and of all their wonderful visits to The Island. He closed his eyes. He could almost feel his grandmother's arm around his neck as they lay in the hammock reading his favourite books.

Flynn sat up straight. His favourite books! Of course! In *Danny the Champion of the World*, Charlie Kinch told a story about putting sugar in the game keepers' petrol tanks to ruin the engines!

Flynn scrambled to his feet.

Outside, the shouting grew louder, and the footsteps were now clearly getting closer to the engine room door. He hadn't a moment to lose!

Flynn grabbed an armful of the bottles and tubes from the workbench. As quickly as he could, he poured and squeezed all of them into the engines. He ran back to the workbench to see what else he could find. The drawers of nuts and bolts caught his eye. He scooped up two handfuls of the smallest ones, and they, too, went into the holes.

He turned wildly. Would it be enough? He took one more desperate look around the room and saw something he hadn't noticed before. In the corner was a small table. A tea tray held a kettle, three mugs, and three round steel containers.

The containers were labelled: Coffee; Tea; Sugar.

Flynn couldn't help himself. He shouted with joy! He sprinted across to the table, grabbed the sugar container, and wrenched off the lid. He emptied half of it into each engine. He could hear the door to the engine room squeaking open. Hurriedly, he screwed the caps back on and flung the sugar container away into the darkness. He then put his hands up and took a few steps backwards, waiting for his captors.

Three men stormed in, each holding a pistol – levelled at Flynn.

"Got you," said one of the guards with obvious pleasure.

It was all over. Flynn held his hands high above his head. The guards viciously jabbed him in the back with their guns as he left the engine room.

Back in the darkness, something moved. The door to a tall storage cupboard swung open and out stepped Briar. The dim light of the phone, still propped against the bench, allowed her to see where she was going.

Silently, she crossed the room, walked up the few stairs to the unlocked door and slipped out into the hallway.

CHAPTER 37

Outside, the wind had risen to a gale. Terrific waves crashed into the side of the ship, throwing sixty-foot plumes of spray into the air and across the deck. Within seconds, Flynn and the guards were soaked through.

The guards marched Flynn to the centre of the deck. They stood around him, stony-faced and silent. Flynn looked up at the bridge. He could see The Pitbull through the window, staring directly at him with a murderous expression on his face.

The Pitbull picked up his gun and calmly opened the door. He descended the stairs to the deck, never once taking his eyes off Flynn. Slowly, as though he was relishing each step, he walked towards him.

The scar on his face glistened in the sea spray. Flynn watched as an evil smile spread across his face.

As The Pitbull made his way across the deck, a tiny movement by the dragon's cages caught Flynn's eye. Squinting against the flying spray, he made out the dark shape of a person. Was it another guard? For an instant, they stepped out into the light, before quickly withdrawing back into the shadows of the towering cages. In that split second, Flynn saw that it was a girl of about his own age, with long, copper-coloured hair. She looked directly at him before retreating back into the darkness.

There was now just twenty feet between Flynn and The Pitbull – twenty feet from certain death! Flynn couldn't bear to look at the ugly grin on The Pitbull's face, so he turned away to look across the vastness of the dark sea. The wind shrieked and the ship pitched from side to side. They were now in a full-scale hurricane.

Flynn closed his eyes and concentrated on the sensation of the sea spray on his face, the wind whipping at his hair. In the midst of the storm, he felt suddenly calm.

CHAPTER 38

When the huge, dark, writhing mass crashed onto the deck directly between Flynn and The Pitbull, it seemed as though the sky had fallen. Everybody reeled backwards in utter confusion; the guards, Flynn, and the advancing Pitbull – no one could understand quite what had happened.

From above, through the howling wind, Flynn heard a wild shout. Paddy! The sound of his brother's voice spurred him into action before anyone else could react. In a split-second, Flynn assessed his options. He saw nine men sprawling in the net and struggling to get free. He saw The Pitbull, his face twisting into an angry snarl. He saw the three dragons locked in their cages. He saw the girl moving around them with the agility of a cat. Behind him, he heard the guards shout in anger. Then, he turned and ran for the edge of the deck.

The loud crack of a rifle sounded above the wind. But there was no impact – The Pitbull had missed him! Not quite believing what he was about to do, Flynn bolted the last few yards to the edge of the ship. With a frightened yell, he leapt over the railing. But it was too high – his foot snagged on the top and it sent him end over end, somersaulting forty feet down into the furious black ocean.

From high above, Elton and Paddy saw Flynn splash down into the sea. The dragon folded his wings against his body and dropped like a thunderbolt. Paddy could see what was about to happen and wriggled towards Elton's head, taking a huge breath and bracing himself.

Dragon and boy entered the ocean like a giant gannet. In just a few seconds, they had descended forty feet below the surface. Paddy opened his eyes. Immediately, he could see what the dragon was thinking – down here, looking up, they could see the deck lights of the Pitbull's ship shining down through the water. It also meant that they might be able to spot his brother.

Elton thrashed to and fro in the deep. The waves and foam made strange shapes above them in the dancing light. Paddy's breath was running out! He tugged on Elton's spines, letting him know that they must soon surface. He saw a dark, motionless shape to his left. It was Flynn! Letting go of Elton, he swam hard, grabbing his brother by the arm and stroking for the surface. But they were still thirty feet under. He knew that he was at the end of his breath. He could feel his mind clouding and the edges of his vision starting to blacken. He was just seconds away from passing out.

Just as Paddy began to lose consciousness, he felt the giant talon of Elton close around him. Water rushed past him like a river, and suddenly he felt the sting of the sea on his cheeks and heard the tremendous crash of the waves. Above him, he could hear the powerful flapping of Elton's wings. He gulped in the sweet air. He was alive! But what about Flynn? He looked across. Elton held his brother in his other talon! Desperately, Paddy looked for signs of life in Flynn, but his body hung motionless. Then, the most amazing sound! Flynn coughed and groaned and a stream of salt water poured from his mouth. He coughed some more, then finally looked over at Paddy.

Paddy laughed with delight.

"You're still a terrible diver!" he yelled to his brother.

Elton flew high above the ship. Paddy could see the men running in all directions. Some looked over the railing while others stared up into the sky. The Pitbull stood motionless in the centre of the deck, staring straight ahead in a daze.

Without warning, Elton suddenly gave a mighty roar, followed by a blazing streak of fire which cut the night sky in two. In that roar Paddy heard all of Elton's hurt and sadness at losing Iris.

Below, the men looked up, startled by the fiery display. They raised their guns and started shooting, but Elton was already hundreds of yards away, invisible in the night sky.

The blind shooting continued for a long time. It was only when The Pitbull finally ordered his men to stop firing that he noticed that the doors on the three dragons' cages were now wide open, and the dragons were gone.

CHAPTER 39

Back on The Island, their mother fussed around the boys, dressing their cuts and bruises with care. Flynn's ribs hurt. He groaned in pain and Ada made little noises of sympathy. Their father listened gravely when the boys retold their story, shaking his head often and marvelling at his sons' bravery and resourcefulness.

But Flynn also felt a terrible sadness. They had failed the three dragons still caged on the deck of The Pitbull's ship. Outside, Elton wailed and roared and tore up the ground. He was missing Iris terribly.

The boys' mother hugged them, trying to cheer them up, when the mournful sound of Elton's wailing suddenly stopped. There was a short silence, followed by the sound of excited roars and muffled thumps.

Worried that Elton may have decided to fly back to The Pitbull's ship to save Iris, Flynn and Paddy ran to the door.

When Paddy opened it, he began to laugh and cheer. On the grass, two dragons rolled over and over in a joyous embrace – Iris and Elton! They purred like gigantic cats and puffed clouds of smoke into the air.

High above, Flynn heard the sound of dragons' roars. They looked up. A bright pink dragon flashed past, followed by a black one. The dragons from the cages! The Pitbull was going home empty handed.

"But how…" Flynn trailed off as he remembered the girl with the red hair.

The two dragons put on a fiery display in the sky before turning towards Dragon's Crater and disappearing into the night.

After Coco finally received her dinner, she curled up in the corner and went to sleep. Occasionally, her legs jerked and she snorted loudly, making them all laugh. Lightning and Clappers, not wanting to miss out, appeared at the window for an affectionate pat.

Meanwhile, Elton and Iris stayed outside, snickering at each other and rubbing their necks together before they, too, finally took off into the night sky.

After a meal of damper and fried eggs cooked over the fire, and two mugs of hot coco each, the children went to bed. Paddy lay down and stretched with pleasure. He began to tell Flynn a joke, but then suddenly fell silent. Flynn looked over. Paddy was sound asleep! That was probably funnier than his joke was likely to be, thought Flynn. He felt Coco climb up and curl herself into a ball at the foot of his bed. He could feel the lovely warmth of her body through the blankets. His own body ached all over. In seconds, Flynn fell into a deep sleep.

CHAPTER 40

The Pitbull drained the last of his coffee. He was tired beyond measure, but forced himself to stay awake. Outside, the storm blew them in the wrong direction – directly away from The Island. No one had been able to tell him what had happened to the ship's anchor.

Behind him, the door opened. The Pitbull turned to see his two ship's engineers enter the bridge. Their hands were black with grease and oil. They shuffled in, looking down at the carpet. They didn't say anything. They didn't have to say a word.

With all his might, The Pitbull flung his cup against the wall, where it shattered into a thousand pieces.

His engineers cowered in the corner as he stalked past them. He cuffed one of them hard across the head. He kicked open the door to the bridge, descended the stairs, and strode across the deck. He mumbled and shouted to himself as he threw open the door to go below. It banged violently in the wind.

The Pitbull descended the stairs in a fury and walked along the corridor towards his quarters, staggering from one side of the corridor to the other in the pitching seas.

Then, he saw it. A lone chicken was carefully making its way across the steel floor. It clucked loudly and fixed him with a beady eye. He hurried past it down the hall. As he neared his quarters, he saw that the door was wide open and light spilled into the hallway. He heard a bleating sound; was that a goat? The Pitbull ran the last few steps.

Reaching the door to his quarters, The Pitbull stared in disbelief. His jaw dropped open. Before him, a dozen hens and several goats looked at him standing in the doorway. A couple of the chickens squawked in surprise and scrambled away. He looked further into the room. Two goats stood on his bed; one of them had already pooped on it. More poop could be seen all over the floor – goat or chicken? He wasn't sure. From the bathroom doorway appeared the head of a chicken, curious about this new visitor.

"Brrrrraaaawk," it squawked.

The Pitbull sank to his knees and began to pound the floor with this fists.

Behind him, deep in the shadows, a smile played across Briar's lips as she ran back to her room.

If you enjoyed reading The Dragon Defenders,
I'd be so grateful if you'd take the time to rate it
or write a review on Amazon.com

Thanks,

www.dragonbrothersbooks.com

Sign up to find out when the next chapter book in the series comes out.

Simply visit **www.dragonbrothersbooks.com** and enter your email address. We'll keep you updated on new books, and we'll send you an email whenever anything cool happens!

About the author

Once, when James Russell was a child, he read a book so exciting it made his heart thump in his chest. Now his aim in life is to write books that will do just that for other children. He hopes that this is one of them.

James lives in Auckland, New Zealand with his wife and two young sons, who love adventure in all its forms.